THE TRUTH ABOUT MAKE-BELIEVE

THE TRUTH ABOUT MAKE-BELIEVE

A NOVEL

Mickey Grubb

.

If you are adopted,

this book is dedicated to you.

We're born alone, we live alone, we die alone. Only through our love and friendship can we create the illusion for the moment that we're not alone.

– Orson Welles

The Truth About Make-Believe

ONE

Standing in the middle of the rear seat, the tiny legs moved quickly from side to side to keep the rest of the body upright and in place as the car made its way through the night over narrow, winding roads. There had to be someone in the car steering it in the right direction although the young boy could not see anyone or hear anyone speak – just frightening silence. The ride was short, but it seemed like an eternity not being able to make sense of it all. While a two year old may not have much depth in understanding, some things are understood through a natural process – instinct.

As sudden as a memory, the motion came to a halt. A light came on, and then extinguished. There was hardly time for his eyes to adjust or focus. Then, as abruptly as before, the light was turned on again as the rear door opened, and a strange man leaned into the cavity, reaching for the child's arm. His hand touched the shirt sleeve, but was unable to secure a grip. The small body quickly retreated to the far side of the car, desperately trying to avoid capture, not really knowing how to evade anything, maneuvering solely on impulse, a sixth sense. Unable to reach the lad without climbing into his space, the silence was broken by words familiar to the child. "Come here, boy," barked the stern voice.

Now frozen by the piercing sound waves, the prey was easily snared without much of a fight. The helpless quarry was swiftly seized, dragged across the seat, a cover

9

flung over his head plunging him into total darkness. He was picked-up and carried away into the night, confused and frightened, feeling helpless and alone. He was you know – alone.

Strange what shit comes to mind when you're crouched in dense tropical undergrowth or elephant grass watching a much traveled trail, waiting for some movement, something to observe and catalog or maybe to shoot; hopefully, the enemy, whoever or whatever in the hell that may be. Sitting quietly alone in this hell hole can scatter your thoughts. I think they call it being scatterbrained. I must have it bad 'cause I often reflect upon memories or thoughts that seem like memories of early childhood, a time of innocence and living carefree without a worry in the world about what tomorrow might hold. But let's face it, there are some things all of us remember and muse about from time to time. Like, the first time we had sex. Then, the first time we had sex with someone we truly love. And here, there's the pong of death that almost takes your breath away; and, conversely, the sweet stench that distinguishes the death of the enemy from that of your fallen comrades. Jesus, I wonder sometimes how we are able to breathe at all.

I remember arriving in the country (simply "in country" as the military likes to put it) of the Republic of South Vietnam on 3 March 1967 at 0630 (6:30 A.M.) just barely eighteen years old; and, as a new arrival, labeled an FNG (fuckin' new guy). No one wants to be an FNG in Nam. But fortunately, or unfortunately, depending on how you look at it, FNG's are everywhere, in every pay grade from private to general. The on-the-job training usually takes around six months to complete and to shed the FNG tag, if lady luck sticks with you that long.

The long flight from Honolulu, Hawaii was making its landing approach for Da Nang. Knots formed in the pit of my stomach as the plane jerked and lurched into a steeper descent. I took a deep breath and swallowed while shifting in my seat to get a view through a porthole. Through the small eyehole just forward of the Boeing 707's port wing, an array of colors streamed past, various shades of green jungle foliage, dull-colored waterways, dirty yellowish rice paddies, the flash of lights from vehicles on Highway 1 and other roads below, grey, dark buildings, and just ahead, the airfield. A stewardess took position at the front of the plane and lifted a microphone from its bracket on the aircraft bulkhead.

"We are on our final approach into Da Nang International Airport." Then the all familiar phrase echoed on thousands of flights every day around the world. "Please return your seats to their full upright position and securely fasten your seat belts. Also, return your table-trays to their upright and locked position. Touchdown will be in approximately three minutes. On behalf of the captain and the crew of Continental Air Services (CASI), we wish you all the luck in the world and hope to see you on a return flight." The irony of her words was lost somewhere in translation by most of the youthful grunts about to embark on a journey into manhood.

Within a few moments, we were jolted forward then slammed backwards, our heads hitting the back of the seats, as the wheels of the aircraft touched down on the runway. It was a rough landing. The plane's engines shifted into reverse thrust, quickly slowing us to a taxi speed. The airliner continued a short distance then turned sharply onto an apron leading to the terminal. The large aircraft slowed even more then braked to a sudden halt. The cabin doors were flung open, and the early morning atmosphere spilled into the cabin. It was my first taste of the fetid air tainted with kerosene and scorching fecal matter carried by an ocean breeze that quickly drove the cabin temperature to well over one hundred degrees. Welcome to Vietnam.

Before we could disengage our seatbelts and standup, an Air Force master sergeant carrying a clipboard and megaphone entered through the doorway. "Alright men, listen up. Good morning, I hope your flight here was enjoyable. I want to welcome each one of you to Da Nang on behalf of the Joint Service Processing Center. I just have a couple of items to go over with you regarding how to debark the plane and where to go once you are inside the terminal."

Boy, I thought, that's all we need, another drawn out briefing about not getting lost inside the terminal while we are roasting in this oven. Others must have had the same thought. I heard someone nearby wearing camouflaged utilities quietly lament, "Screw you Sarge. It's like a furnace in here! Let's get the hell off this aircraft!"

The JTO's (Joint Transportation Officer) voice faded to a faint whisper as the aircraft's engines continued to whine. Sweat-soaked green fatigues and camouflaged uniforms filled the aisles. Bodies jostled for position while reaching for their carry-on items from the overhead storage compartments. Outside, the ground crew moved hurriedly about unloading the cargo bays and carefully servicing the plane. Through the window I could see uniformed men standing at a distance in the shade of the terminal waiting anxiously to board the aircraft. They were going home. Inside, the master sergeant finished his instructional speech on how to exit the plane and where to go once we were inside the terminal. Not much of what he said was understood above all the commotion. I remained seated in my window seat patiently waiting for my opportunity to join the slow moving exodus.

Finally, I made my way up the aisle and through the hatch into the bright, unsympathetic morning sun, pausing momentarily. I continued along the debarkation ramp into the terminal. The signs directing the way to the baggage claim area were surprisingly easy to follow. Upon reaching the claim area, the wait for the retrieval of my two bags was relatively short. The only complaint I recall having, besides the damn heat, was that the two bags weighed far more than what I remembered when they were checked Stateside.

On my way to the baggage claim area, I had spotted the First Marine Division plaque hanging from the overhead. With my duffel bag (loaded with iron) and val-pack, I headed for the counter located just beneath the 1st Mar Div sign where a sea of green and camouflaged uniforms were tussling with their baggage with documents stuck under their arms, inching closer to the counter, one baby-step at a time. The green fatigues of Marines coming in country from CONUS (Continental United States) seemed to slightly outnumber the camouflaged uniforms of those returning from R&R (rest and recuperation). I fell in line and began the familiar military "hurry up and wait" process of checking-in. Several minutes passed. Finally, I moved in front of the counter facing a Marine Corporal. We exchanged cordial pleasantries as I handed over my paperwork.

"Good morning, Corporal. I have orders to report to First Recon Battalion."

The corporal took my orders, removed his copy, and stamped an endorsement at the top of the first page and handed them back to me. "You're all set to go. Looks like you are being assigned to a special recon team. You are the third Marine that I have processed this morning with the same MOS (military occupational specialty). Grab your bags and take a seat over there on one of those benches under the "reserved seating" sign. A truck will be by to pickup you and the others from that area in about ninety minutes."

I gathered my gear and made my way through the growing wave of sweaty green fatigues to one of the benches in the reserved area. There was one sign above the location marked for officers and another labeled simply as "all others." I introduced myself to a couple of Marines relaxing on one of the bench-made seats. There was L/CPL (Lance Corporal) Dan LaPont from New Orleans, Louisiana and L/CPL Kevin Sparks from Baltimore, Maryland, who reminded me a lot of my childhood friend, Flick. His smile, a crooked smile with parted lips twisted to one side of his face, and slightly raised eyebrows matched the facial expression of Flick to a tee. Unbelievable. Ironically, all three of us had orders to report to First Recon. L/CPLs LaPont and Sparks had gone through BRC (Basic Reconnaissance Course) together at Camp Pendleton in San Diego. My BRC training was conducted at Camp Lejeune with the Second Force Recon Company. We had the training but absolutely no combat experience. However, we were gung-ho FNG's and eager to get started on that experience detail.

It's funny how experience teaches the reality of things. Now with over ten months together in the field, there's one thing for certain we've learned that's real. This jungle, the bush, is a real motherfucker.

For the longest time, I thought the whole episode of the little child riding in the car through the darkness was just some sort of peculiar, mysterious dream I had had. But, when I was about fifteen years old, I had a conversation with my dad regarding the earliest memories that each of us could recall. I could easily remember events from when I was four and five years old – even one or two things that happened when I was three. But both dad and I were surprised when I related what I thought was an old dream. Dad explained that it was no dream. The ride was real.

"That was the night your mother and I got

you…when we were adopting you, at age two."

We all have things from our past that we return to now and then, to work on or think over, things from the past and present that require our attention. It may be some insecurity about our physical appearance, or a relationship to a friend or relative, or maybe something as simple as striking out with the bases loaded in Little League. And, in the course of growing up, each of us encounters situations and circumstances that will mold and shape us as individuals. These events become part of our inner being. Some issues are dealt with and forgotten, while others are stored away to be revisited at some later date.

Adoption is one of those issues whose meaning will change with each visitation. To some, these are trivial matters while to others they are concerns to be hidden away in a corner of the heart destined for some future rendezvous.

TWO

Corporal Michael Anthony Gennaro was not Italian as his name might suggest. Michael was adopted by relatives, an Italian family, after his parents were killed in an automobile crash when he was two years old. His mother's sister, Michael's aunt, married Anthony Gennaro before Michael was born, and they were asked by Mike's parents to be his god parents when his mother realized she was going to have a baby. I learned all this from Michael in just a little over two weeks of having known him. We met the same day that L/Cpl's LaPont, Sparks, and I were sent to Camp Carroll from our brief stop at Da Nang.

Corporal Gennaro and I exchanged adoption stories while being teamed together to help build or fix radio bunkers when we weren't doing something else. We were both intrigued with the journey that each of us had had to this point in our lives. Although the circumstances surrounding our adoptions were different, there were enough similarities to connect us and to form a strong friendship in a short period of time. We promised each other to stay in touch when we finally made it back home after our tours were completed. Just another round of make-believe...

Camp Carroll is situated on a plateau with valleys all around it, and the two sides north and west have short valleys that rise to mountainous terrain. LaPont, Sparks, and I were supposed to be at Carroll only a short period of time before beginning special recon missions in unspecified areas in and around the DMZ (demilitarized zone). After two weeks in camp, we hadn't done much of anything but build bunkers. The day's mission was supposed to be just a walk into one of those valleys not far from the perimeter. Just a routine jaunt to check out the area to make sure nobody was around maybe checking us out, setting traps, being a nuisance. None of us expected to see anyone. And, even if we did happen to encounter someone lurking in the brush, we expected him to run like hell when we approached. After all, these gooks do not like to fight in the daylight.

This was the first real mission for L/CPLs LaPont, Sparks, and me. Second Lieutenant Hampton Taylor was in command of the patrol, but First Sergeant Marvin Cox called all the shots. The Lieutenant had only been in country for a little over a month. Sarge was half way through his second tour.

The patrol began at 0600 hours. We had only been out for a couple of hours when we heard a sudden "pop" that sounded a lot like a firecracker exploding. We all dropped to the ground. No one made a sound. We were trying to get a fix on where the pop had originated.

Sergeant Cox broke the silence. "Anyone know where that shot came from?"

No one said a word. Then three shots rang out in succession off to my right.

"I got the son of a bitch, Sarge!" yelled LaPont. "He must have been a sniper...and a dumb ass at that. He jumped up and started to run. I shot him, Sarge. I tried to hit him in the ass."

"Okay, LaPont...you and Sparks come with me. Let's check it out. Approach with caution," the Sarge warned.

"Is everyone okay?" Lt. Taylor asked.

"Gennaro ain't moving. I think he's hit," said Private First Class Newman.

He laid just to my right. I instinctively moved quickly to him, arriving about the same time as Navy Corpsman Hickman. Corporal Gennaro had taken a round through his lower back. The shell had exited the stomach leaving a hole in his abdomen the size of a cantaloupe. I sat down next to him and took his head in my hands. I crossed my legs and carefully slid them under the Corporal's head.

"It's going to be alright," I said as Corpsman Hickman began his assessment.

The young Corporal's eyes were not focused. At first he said nothing as he looked up at me. I didn't think he could see me. His head appeared to be okay, but his stomach had a gaping hole in it. Most of his intestines were lying on his crotch area.

"Is it bad, man? Am I going to die?" Corporal Gennaro asked looking up at me. The look on my face was probably more frightening than encouraging. I know he looked shitless. His fatigue jacket and uniform were matted with blood. I held his head on my lap as the corpsman worked around his wound. He was just going through the motions, applying his medical training as best he could.

"Hell no, you're not going to die!" I said trying to give him some sort of hope as I looked into his sunken eyes. This Marine was bleeding to death in my arms and no amount of bandages and pressure was going to stop it.

Corporal Michael Anthony Gennaro's last words were the very words all of us live with every day while in this God forsaken place. It is the question all Marines ask themselves the first thing when waking up, and the last thing they ask before closing their eyes in sleep, whenever that may occur. "Am I going to die in this dirty, rotten, humid, shit-faced jungle, thousands of miles from nowhere?" I wondered as the Corporal drew his last breath.

Corporal Gennaro was only three weeks away from going home.

The detail reached the downed sniper. He wasn't moving and appeared to be dead. "Check him out, LaPont," ordered Sgt. Cox. As L/CPL LaPont approached the body, the gook rolled over and kicked at LaPont striking him on the ankle. LaPont stumbled forward and fell on top of the little maggot, squirming like a worm on a hot city sidewalk trying to escape the burning heat and certain death. LaPont impulsively removed his K-bar from its sheath, and being the skilled surgeon that he is, struck a quick and fatal blow. As it turned out, the sniper had only been grazed by one of LaPont's rounds and had fallen down playing possum in hopes we might move on and leave him there in the bush alone.

"That was a slick move, LaPont," Sgt. Cox said with a firm look of approval in his eyes. "You really know how to handle that weapon. One of the best I've ever seen." From that day forward, L/CPL Dan LaPont from the Big Easy became known as "Dan the K-bar man."

Corporal Gennaro was from Brooklyn, New York. His death was the first casualty that LaPont, Sparks, and I had seen since arriving in country. The sight of blood, especially the blood covering the face of the gook combatant, seemed to charge the senses like an electrical shock. I wanted to see more of those vermin bleed.

The company commander accepted Lieutenant Taylor's and First Sergeant Cox's report on the incident and later that afternoon briefed the battalion commander, Lieutenant Colonel Charles T. Cobb. Lt. Col. Cobb was a respected commander. After his briefing, he lived up to his well deserved esteem by setting aside normal protocol and addressing each one of us personally. The Lieutenant Colonel was due to go state side in about thirty days. He said he had never been to Brooklyn, but he promised us he would personally pay a visit to the family of Corporal Gennaro. For me, there was a certain irony in what he said, but his words meant a lot to each of us.

THREE

I was eight years old when my parents told me I was adopted. I don't think they really wanted to tell me. Maybe it was their sense of knowing right from wrong, I don't know. But something convinced them they had to let me know. It all started at school in the third grade. Many of the kids talked about their older brothers and sisters, and about some of the times they shared together as a family. I was often asked why I didn't have any brothers or sisters. Well, how the hell could I answer that? So, I asked my parents to explain. At first they hesitated, probably thinking I would forget about it. Hey, kids in the third grade don't forget anything. If you are different in any way than the rest of the group, you're going to hear about it, over and over again.

One Friday afternoon after school, my mother and father asked me to sit down in the living room of our house. They had something important to discuss with me. Needless to say, I was frightened. What did I do? The garbage had been taken out, and the dog had been fed. What was it?

My father began by saying, "Son, this matter of brothers and sisters…uh…well, how do I say this? Son, you are adopted."

Man that hit me like a ton of bricks. What was he saying? Adopted? He could tell by my bewildered look I had no idea what he was talking about.

"Your father died when you were almost two, and your mother was unable to take care of you and three other children by herself. She did not have a job or anyone to help her. So, a social worker came to your house and placed you, your sisters and brother into the custody of the state. In other words, the care for you became the responsibility of the state and was no longer that of your mother. Each of you were then taken to a new home where you would have something good to eat and a warm bed to sleep in at night. A Judge, like in a court room, decided that it was best for you to go live with us. That's how we were able to adopt you," he explained, putting it into plain words.

My mom asked me if I had any questions. "Uh, you mean I really do have sisters and a brother?" I nervously asked.

"Yes, you do. Maybe it can be arranged for you to visit with one or more of them if you want to?" she explained. "That is, if we can locate any of them."

"Of course I want to see them," I replied enthusiastically. "When can I go?"

"It may take some time to arrange, but we will work it out as soon as possible," they promised.

The excitement of the moment opened the gates, and a flood of questions came spilling out. I asked, "What was my real mother like? Was she pretty? Was she sad to see us taken from her? What happened to her, and where is she now? Will I ever be able to see her or go to live with her again?"

My adoptive mom was clearly uncomfortable with my barrage of questions. I think she was surprised I asked about my birth mother so quickly. I believe it was the words "real mom" that set her back, but she managed a rather labored reply, "I don't know anything about her. That woman doesn't really matter anyway because I'm your mother now. Do you have any more questions?"

"No, not really," I said trying to hide my disappointment and holding back the tears. Given the tone of her voice, that was enough. I never asked my adopted mom about my birth mother again.

It still wasn't clear to me what being adopted really meant. And at that time, I was afraid to ask. I must have been in shock. Suddenly, the word adopted had become like a disease and had to be whispered. I figured my classmates at school were right after all. I was different. I wasn't sure if that was a good thing or a bad thing. For a moment, the thought of possibly seeing my sisters and brother replaced the shock and awe of being told I was adopted with a feeling of exhilaration and anticipation. If I could visit them, even just one of them from time to time, it would be almost as good as living with them. I could barely wait to tell all of my friends I did have a brother and two sisters. Maybe, I wasn't so different after all. But there was still a lingering dismay, a feeling of being alone.

Over the years I have come to understand that for many adoptees, that's how it is with the issue of adoption, like it or not. But more disturbing, at least I think for me, is the lingering consternation that grips your soul when you're told you are adopted without any in-depth detail regarding the event. You wonder how things would have worked out if you had not been adopted. Your thoughts search deeply for the truth about why it all happened in the first place. Your heart tells you that not everything you were told is exactly the way it was.

Dad's simple explanation became an emotionally laden, complex issue. There were questions like, "Where is my mother now?" "Why didn't the Judge or the court help her to keep us?" I no longer felt free to ask these questions given the previous response by my adoptive mom. Going forward, these questions would have to be examined only in the solitude of self-reflection. Yet, I wasn't angry with my adoptive parents. I knew they loved me and wanted me. If not, then why did I have so many toys, clothes, a dog, and my own bedroom? I have always had, and will always have, tremendous gratitude for having been raised by loving and generous parents.

Suddenly, there was this eerie feeling like a lack of connection, a most disquieting loneliness. I had no sense of history and no claim to my adoptive family. I felt like a stranger in an unfamiliar place. It didn't matter anymore that my adoptive father was highly intelligent and had twenty some patents to his name, that my uncle was an inventor, or that my adopted mother's father, my grandfather, was a legendary law officer. "These people are not my people, and their heritage has no connection to my heritage," were the pounding thoughts inside my head. The emotional mixture of excitement, sadness, and confusion was like trying to put together a million-piece puzzle with all of the pieces turned upside down.

While dealing with the pain of adoption-related loss is a lifetime process, having supportive friends helped ease the difficulties with the emotional storms. My childhood friends were great, and together we developed a nurturing environment for each other's growing pains, both real and perceived. I have found that same brotherhood spirit here in the Corps.

I never realized how much time I had spent thinking about my family situation until I arrived in this disheartening place. But at least here I am with genuine brothers like Dan and Kevin. We are not blood brothers by birth but blood brothers just the same – Marines that would die for each other in a New York minute. That's an indisputable love. Semper Fi.

FOUR

I don't think most adults, not even the highly educated, have really considered how a child is affected by the adoption process. Oh I know there are probably studies of record or some being conducted that measure the affects of adoption on a child. But I'm referring to my situation, one that I know better than anyone else (does). I was two years old when taken from a mother and siblings, people who had been my caregivers, and an environment that had become familiar to me. A bond had been formed. There was a natural sense of security already in place through the relationship with those persons closest to me for those first two years and the surroundings that made up my world. Unlike a newborn, I had a memory and was able to recall meaningful moments from the past. Now there was a period of grieving (although I didn't know what it was called) that had to be experienced, alone. No social worker of the time or any judge pushing paperwork through some courtroom had a clue to the psychosomatic development phases of a child. Even though the memories faded, the attachment to the past was linked through yearnings and emotional feelings that something was different, and I had no way of explaining or understanding what I was experiencing.

At age two, the "terrible twos," language was starting to expand and words were taking on meaning and association. I imagine, after reading about other two year olds in an adoptive family setting, that my favorite words were "no" and "me." The ability to think symbolically had begun to develop. Why was I here among strangers? Who were these people wanting me to call them mom and dad?

Dad was born in 1907. He was the second oldest of five boys and one girl, the youngest. His family was a working class clan with only three of the six children finishing high school. Fifty percent was pretty good for that time in history. If you were not lucky enough to be born into money, most boys and many of the females left school around the age of fifteen and went to work to help the entire family to survive.

Times were hard then. My dad went to work with his father in the coal mines the day after turning fifteen. He told me it was exciting to be working and having a part in supporting his family. He was making a whopping one dollar a shift and an extra five cents for each one ton coal car he and his dad could load and get to the outside before the end of their shift. They worked ten-hour days, six days a week. He could hardly wait to draw his first pay check.

My grandfather died in the mines from a heart attack when dad was nineteen. Dad retrieved a pocket watch from his dad's coveralls just before the body was transported to the surface. It was the only thing my dad had that belonged to his father. He kept it in a safe place and often wound it and set it to the correct time. It was interesting to see him drift to a different place and time when he held that old watch in his hands.

My dad's mother was a very sweet and kind individual. Her house was situated on Premier Mountain next to the main highway, route 52 that connected Welch to the Roderfield/Big Sandy area where I would eventually live. The front yard was small, but open, no fences. So for a young boy, supervision was always, well most of the time, provided whenever I was allowed to play there.

Once while chasing my cousin Seth (I barely knew

him at the time) in a game of tag, I ran across a pile of old lumber, flooring boards that had been ripped from one of the rooms that one of my uncles was remodeling for grandma. Even with supervision, no one issued any decrees or warnings about possible old nails that could be protruding through some of the boards. Naturally, if there's a nail to be found, a young lad will be the one to find it, the needle in the hay stack so to speak. Not only was I the one to discover a nail, I found it with the bottom of my left foot by stepping on it and pushing the rusty spike through my tennis shoe into my flesh approximately one inch. I don't recall the sudden intrusion hurting all that much, but it did cause me to lose my balance and fall. In spite of the wound, before anyone could react, I simply jumped to my feet and continued to pursue Seth. I was determined to catch him. However, after several strides there was a squishing sound coming from my left shoe with each footstep. My foot felt moist, and as I looked down at my foot, I saw that my white sock had turned red. Mom must have seen it about the same time because she came screaming from the front porch in my direction.

"What have you done to yourself?" she asked succinctly.

"He's stepped on a nail, and it's gone into his foot," dad quickly interjected knowing exactly what the situation was.

Well, that started a heated discussion between mom and dad on the merits of holding a safety meeting before an accident happens, not afterwards. Each one was blaming the other for allowing me to play around the stacked lumber in the first place. That's when grandma took over and settled everyone down. She had dad to carry me into the house and place me on the couch in the living room. Grandma then removed my shoe and sock to triage the injury like a nurse in an emergency room. She cleaned the wound and applied an ointment and bandage.

"There," she said. "You're going to be just fine."

By now, mom and dad were back to normal…almost. It was time to leave so everyone said their good-byes and off we went. But we didn't go straight home. Mom told dad to stop at the hospital where she worked. She took me into the emergency room while dad parked the car. Mom knew the doctor and nurses on call that day and explained what had happened. The next thing I knew, the doctor was sticking a nine inch needle into my arm.

"Ouch," I said. It was the only word that came to mind at the moment.

"It's a tetanus shot," he explained as if I knew what the hell he was talking about. "The shot will keep you from getting a serious infection and becoming very ill," he continued. "This shot is good for five years. That's a good thing, right?" he stated rhetorically. While the doctor was singing the praises of the tetanus shot, I was thinking how much more the long needle hurt than the rusty old nail.

But my fondest memories of being with grandma were when I was around the age of three or four, and we would be at her house when no one else was visiting at the same time. She would take me with her to the kitchen and let me pick anything I wanted to eat from the refrigerator, cabinets, or pantry. I always chose the Domino's sugar, and she would gladly give me a cup full along with a spoon to help transfer the granular substance from the container to my watering mouth. It was so good. Of course, mom and dad would object to the tasty treat, but grandma always had the last word. She treated me special because she was. She died when I was five. I cried for days.

My uncles were all friendly, but they hardly ever visited one another. They would get together from time to time at grandma's house. After their mother passed away, one uncle continued to live in the house, but he referred to it as his mother's home. We would sometimes stop in for a short visit on Sunday's as did the other boys of the family. All of my uncles were nice towards me...all except Uncle Dustan. He was only friendly when others were around. I have no idea why he never liked me. I guess that's one of the impossibilities of life, making someone like you.

My dad's sister was somewhat strange. In fact, she was just plain crazy. There was a fixed, wild look in her eyes, and she would say the strangest things that drew some wild looks of their own from other family members. But no one ever said that she was crazy or anything. Or at least nothing was ever said in front of us kids. She had two sons both of whom were much older than me. Each of them committed suicide.

Mom also grew up in a large family. There were eleven children: four girls and seven boys. One of mom's sisters died at the age of five from pneumonia. Mom was born in 1917 and was only seven years of age when her father was killed in the line of duty. He was part of a special group of government agents that were later referred to as G-men. At the time, three of her brothers and one sister were married and no longer lived at home.

Her mother was a tough individual in her own right with an appearance much like what I envisioned how the women of the early frontier must have looked. She raised the remaining six children residing at home on her own, teaching each the merits of hard work on their small farm on Belcher Mountain near the town of Welch. Grandmother sold the farm and moved to her home on Virginia Street in Welch in the late thirties a few years before the start of World War II.

My favorite aunt of all was mom's baby sister, Melinda. Everyone called her Mel. My Aunt Mel was pretty on the outside and on the inside. She always had a smile. She called me her second son. She had a son, the oldest, and three daughters all of whom were my favorite cousins. Age wise, I was closest to the youngest and always felt like I could have been their brother anytime we were together. We all loved each other very much. We still do.

Before meeting and marrying my mom, dad was married once before. He and his first wife had a son who was named after my adoptive father. The marriage didn't last but a few years and ended in divorce when she ran off with another man. She took their son with her, and dad never really fought it because he worked so much. It would have been difficult to raise a child without someone to care for him while dad was away ten to twelve hours a day, six days a week. Dad never spent a lot of time with his son.

My half brother was much older than me. He was old enough to be my father. We really never had a meaningful relationship. I think dad deeply regretted he had not pursued the opportunity to be a closer father for his son. I don't think he missed the woman. He was glad that bitch was gone. He met and married my mom after his son, Junior, was grown.

Mom, on the other hand, had also been married once but had no children. She was married for only about a year when her husband stopped by grandma's house after work one evening to pick-up mom. Grandma had been fighting the common cold that had turned into the flu. Mom and Aunt Mel spent the day helping with some needed chores. They washed clothes and cleaned the house thoroughly for grandma. They also prepared a meal and were planning to eat before mom and her first husband departed for their home located approximately five miles away. However, when her husband arrived and entered the kitchen, he pulled a hand gun and started shooting. One bullet hit mom in the abdomen. She collapsed onto the floor. He fired a round in the direction of Aunt Mel who dove for cover beside a cabinet and then crawled quickly into an adjoining bedroom. She was not hit.

It's not clear what really happened next. As the official story goes, grandma heard the shots while sitting on the edge of her bed just moments before she planned to go into the kitchen to prepare for the meal. Not knowing what was actually happening, she grabbed my grandfather's pearl handled Colt 45 pistol she always kept near the bed, loaded. She moved cautiously into the short hallway between her bedroom and the kitchen. There she saw mom's husband with a pistol in his hand aiming it at my mother still unconscious on the floor. Grandma quickly fired a round in the direction of her son-in-law striking him in the side just below the arm pit. He was knocked off his feet and landed on his back on the floor several feet from my mom. Realizing he had been shot, he then placed the barrel of his gun into his mouth, pulled the trigger, and blew off the top of his head. He committed suicide without revealing why he had tried to kill my mom and my aunt.

The unofficial version of the story, as told to me by one of my uncles, was that the police report surmised that mom's husband was drunk (from whiskey) and entered the house angry, firing his pistol. Thinking he had killed his wife, he then turned the gun on himself and kissed this world good-bye. There was no mention of grandma's shot. A friend of the family who worked at the funeral home where the body was taken said that the son of a bitch had been shot three times with three different caliber shells. Oddly enough, those details were not mentioned in the newspaper account that matched grandma's story.

So, I can understand how eager both my mom and dad were to adopt a child. The clock was ticking, and they may have never had another opportunity after this one, after me. I can see why even the mere mention of the word adoption can be confusing to both a child and adults.

FIVE

The hills of southern West Virginia are really rugged mountain ranges much like the Alps in Switzerland only on a miniature scale. West Virginia's nickname the "Mountain State" is certainly appropriate. Though many of its mountain ranges may be termed "hills," there are more than a few that have peaks exceeding four thousand feet above sea level. In fact, the entire state is locked within and is part of the bigger mountainous region, the Appalachian Mountains. Per square mile, the state has more mountain land than any other state. Some say, if all the mountains in West Virginia were flattened, the state would be as large as Texas.

Between the towering anomalous heights supported by uneven sides and overhanging cliffs are narrow, winding valleys that occasionally open to a mantle of soft, green colored fields of unrivaled, bravura beauty. Beneath these grand and majestic hills, in almost every grotto and crevice, lies a treasure, a cache of black gold that has provided a reward for the assiduous groups of characters that settled and continue to inhabit this austere territory and choose to risk their health and lives to supply the nation and indeed, much of the world with its prize of fossil fuel – coal. McDowell County was once called the Nation's Coal Bin because of its extensive bituminous coal reserves. Throughout the 1940's and 50's, the county and surrounding region led the world annually in coal shipments to various parts of the globe for use in the manufacturing of steel and for producing electricity.

I grew up in a place named Big Sandy, referred to by some as Roderfield, a larger adjacent area where some people maintained a post office box mailing address. Big Sandy is one of many small communities nestled in the valleys of McDowell County in southern West Virginia that were originally established by the coal companies to provide housing for their employees and families. These communities are often referred to as coal camps.

My house resembled a majority of the other houses, a large four-room stucco house consisting of a living room, kitchen and dining room combination, and two bedrooms. Only a few of the houses had an inside toilet or bathroom facility. Most had outside toilets called outhouses or sometimes referred to as shithouses. My dad added a bathroom to our house when I was about seven years old. We moved into the house when I was five. In just two short years, our family managed to not only keep up with, but surpass the Jones'.

The winters were usually cold with plenty of snow. All of the houses were heated by coal stoves or coal furnaces. The summers were hot. Hardly anyone had air-conditioning in their homes. Window and oscillating fans circulated hot air throughout the entire structure. At least there was air movement between the rooms.

Big Sandy's roads were all dirt except for the asphalt pavement cutting through the center of the neighborhood, the only opening to the outside world. Oaks, poplars, and fruit trees, mostly apple, shaded nearly everyone's yards. There was a baseball field nearby where most boys between the ages of eight and eighteen spent many of their summer days. Not every family had a television set. Most families gathered around a radio for their evening entertainment, listening to the Grand Ole

Opry broadcast from Nashville, Tennessee.

The county was dry, which meant that bootleggers or moonshiners thrived, especially in outlying towns like Big Sandy. There were two grade schools in our community, one for whites and one for the colored, which was really about two miles away and not actually located inside the camp.

The nearest real town outside of Big Sandy was Welch, located approximately eight to ten miles north of Big Sandy. Welch was the county seat and center of government and shopping activities. In Welch there was a public swimming pool where the only blue and clear water in the region could be found. The local children did cannonballs and jack-knives in the deep end. We poor Roderfield kids did cannonballs and dives from the "big rock" into the coal-black Tug Fork River. Its waters not only carried coal dust out of the county but also a boat-load of crap and other trash that floated serenely in the shadows of the steep-rugged mountains through the valleys to places beyond the county line.

Most people in the county did not interact with people outside of their individual communities. Social life and activities were contained to primarily the workplace, school, and church except for a few civic events like fairs or parades held at various times of the year that attracted the participation of many of the county's population. In addition, communities also supported the sports programs of the county's nine high schools, five white and four colored.

Big Sandy had two churches. One was a snake-handling church where the majority of the congregation was made-up of outsiders. Those from our neighborhood who attended church went to the Church of God, a holy-roller church where hell fire and damnation were preached every Wednesday evening and two services on Sunday.

What a childhood – growing up with good friends, giving each other strength, courage, hope, and cherished memories. We learned from each other the difference between good and evil.

In the summer of 1954 not long after we moved into the camp, when I was five and about to turn six, my mom took me to Big Sandy Grade School to register for entry into the first grade. There were other parents there with their children and some without, all standing in line waiting for the doors to open and registration to begin. It was an exciting occasion – starting school for the first time and a chance to meet kids my own age that I had certainly never before seen.

It was there under the hot August sun around 10:00 a.m. when I first saw him. He was holding a football when our eyes first met, seeing beyond our years. Catching the flying missile surprised him. We smiled. That was how Flick and I met. He was one of the first and best friends to ever enter my life. He and his mother were also there to register Flick for the first grade.

"We'll go to school together. We'll be best friends," Flick joyfully announced.

It was thrilling to have a new friend who also happened to own a football and would bring it every day to school for us to pass (throw) and catch and to have all kinds of fun. School was going to be exhilarating. But, Flick was a dreamer, we both would soon find out.

When the process of registering was over, everyone returned to his or her home. School did not actually begin until after Labor Day. That was almost a whole month away. I couldn't wait to have another chance to catch and throw Flick's football. I told mom about my new friend and how much fun we had playing on the school ground while she was busy getting me signed-up. That's when she explained that Flick would not be going to school with me during the coming year. He had to attend another school located about two miles away. She said that maybe Flick and I would get to go to the same school next year if everything worked out. I did not understand why he had to go to another school when there was this school so much closer to where he lived. He would have to ride a school bus to get to his school. It didn't seem fair.

Finally, the first day of school arrived. I was up early that morning full of energy. Quickly, I consumed a bowl of oatmeal, a piece of toast with grape jelly, a glass of orange juice, and a glass of milk. I also forced down a purple rabbit-shaped vitamin and managed to brush my teeth and comb my hair without having to be reminded. Mom did, however, go over a list of last minute instructions just to be sure I knew where to go and what to do upon arrival at the school. I would walk to school in a group with the Wilson twins, Mary and Martha, Howard Davis, a boy who lived a few houses from ours, and my cousin, known affectionately as Seth. We would saunter through several adjoining neighborhood yards that led to the rear of the school without having to encounter automobile traffic along the way. We would not make any detours. Upon reaching the destination, I was to go straight to my classroom and check-in with the teacher for my seating assignment. These instructions were repeated. Mom wanted to be sure that I understood the plan.

The classroom was full of movement, laughter, high-pitched talking, sneezing, coughing, and other weird sounds that only a bunch of first graders could understand. Taunting the nostrils was an assortment of aromas such as the smell of new tennis shoes (PF Flyers no doubt), chalk, old books, bubblegum (which was swiftly confiscated by the teacher), child-flavored perspiration, and of course, farts, the silent kind at first. By the end of the day, the farting decibel level rose a hundredfold, echoing throughout the room and down the hallways, bouncing off walls, blowing open the doors to the outside world and springing into outer space. The teacher spent most of the first day teaching us some of her favorite expressions: be quiet, shut up, sit-down, get in your seat, no you may not go to the bathroom, no you may not talk to your neighbor, don't throw that spit wad, stop that, what part of no do you not understand.

Recess was an enjoyable break from the grueling learning curve. It gave us an opportunity to meet some of our classmates, learn their names, talk, and play together. Of particular interest were the Web brothers, Tommy and Kenneth. Tommy was a year older than Kenneth, but had been held back for another round of the first grade. They were destined to be the bullies of our grade as they proudly announced that they could and would kick anybody's ass they wanted. And we all believed them. Of course, ass was one of many new words I learned that day. Damn was another word with a dual meaning I heard at some point during each recess. It didn't always refer to a huge cement wall holding back the flow of a river. Hell and hells-bells were other cool expressions that could liven up a conversation and frequently sprung from the lips of some of the more school-experienced boys. Realizing the meaning of most of the words, I stored all of them away into my memory bank for future reference. I was sure each one would come in handy one day. There was also a girl that was very noticeable and educed many snickers behind her back. She had the brightest red hair I had ever seen and her face, arms, and legs were densely festooned with varying shades and sizes of brown spots commonly known as freckles. I don't remember her real name, but her nickname was Snooky. She looked so much like Howdy Doody that she could have passed for his twin sister. Snooky spent the entire recess chasing after several boys threatening to smear a slimy bugger, freshly picked from her hog-like nasal cavity, all over their faces if she caught them. I made sure there was always plenty of distance between her position and my location.

The first day passed quickly. None of us had to tell our parents about our first day at school. Ms. Pridemore promised to tell each of our parents for us. How nice of her to do that. And, I didn't remember much about reading, writing, or arithmetic on the first day, but I was sure we were all on the right path for a good education.

The one thing I do remember about Ms. Pridemore was her compassion for her students. She loved each one of us equally and often told us so. I liked that. Once after I had had a bad day both in the classroom and on the playground at recess, she had a one-on-one talk with me. I guess she saw that I was feeling down and sad (maybe guilty) with the way my day was going and wanted to share some of her compassion with me. She reminded me that we all have bad days sometime in our lives. It happens to all of us sooner or later.

"No one," Ms. Pridemore softly spoke, "has a perfect day every day."

I frowned and then exclaimed, "I wish I was grown-up! Being a kid sure does suck."

"A lot of boys want to hurry up and become men. But, there comes a time when they wish they could be boys again. A boy's life passes very quickly as it is. I can tell you a secret," she said. "Do you want to hear it?"

I nodded. "Yes, what is it?"

She leaned in very close to me and whispered with the sweetest breath I had ever smelled, "People don't really grow-up. They may look grown-up, but it's not real. It's only make-believe. Men and women remain children in their hearts and souls. They want to run and play, but are prevented from doing so by the weight of the grown-up disguise they wear. They'd like to take off their concealing cloak and return to the ball fields and playgrounds, if only for a few moments. They would like nothing better than to return home after a long, hard day at play to a waiting mom and dad who will nurse the cuts and bruises and comfort their wounded feelings. I have seen many boys and girls grow into men and women. But I want you to remember one thing – growing older is not a choice, but growing up is."

I didn't really catch the meaning of what Ms. Pridemore was saying at the time. I do now. Ms. Pridemore's secret is now my own.

When the final bell rang, we all scampered from the classroom like circus animals darting for freedom before the doors to the cages could be tightly secured. Six grades of children spilled out onto the school grounds like water breaking through the face of a dam. Some headed for the bus stop while others lingered momentarily, spreading out to many locations on the playground, getting to know newly found friends. Looking toward the bus stop, I saw a familiar face, smiling, waving both hands in the air, and calling out my name. It was my friend Flick. The same buses that had arrived to pick up the students from our school had delivered the kids from the other school to their drop-off point. Flick had exited the bus and stopped to tie his shoe when he noticed that I was nearby. His football was lying there on the ground next to his lunch box. Without delay, Flick picked up the inflated pig's bladder and gave it a heave. I ran a few steps and grasped the projectile firmly between my hands. We smiled.

That was the beginning of what would become an after-school routine. Before the end of the year, Flick and I were also playing on the school grounds on the weekends. Our friendship was so natural, having grown from a brief encounter to one of inseparable pals.

SIX

The day commenced just like most Saturdays: out of bed around 8:00 a.m., hurry to the bathroom, take a leak, wash the hands, brush the teeth, go to the living room sofa, but first turn on the TV, find a cartoon program or western, wait for breakfast. However, this particular day was different. I was up at 8:00 a.m. as usual, but this time breakfast was ready and waiting for me. I finished in the bathroom and sat down at the kitchen table. Mom poured a glass of milk and a glass of orange juice to go with my meal. There were pancakes, biscuits and gravy, scrambled eggs, bacon, and a sliced tomato. I had some of each. So did dad. I enjoyed a big breakfast; however, that usually meant mom and dad had a long day planned, which included a trip to grandma's, a haircut for me, and a long, dull stop at the Kroger store for groceries. Damn. Perfect time for using one of the new words housed in my growing lingua franca. What an exciting day for an eight-year old boy. I could hardly wait to get started – not. I loathed grocery shopping. It destroyed the whole day. But, just before I started to gag myself, mom made an unexpected announcement.

"Today is the day you get to meet your sister, your real-to-life sister."

"Hell's bells, what a great surprise," my reaction interjecting more of the new patois. I didn't think this day would ever arrive. It seemed like an eternity since I had been told my sister and I were adopted and someday I would actually get to meet her. A sentiment of excitement came over me like it was Christmas Day. I had to make another trip to the bathroom. Mom said she would call my sister's mother later in the morning and find out what time we could drop by. In the meantime, I was to do some chores, like take out the trash, feed Spot, and pick out the clothes I wanted to wear. That wasn't hard. I only had one good pair of jeans. Surely she didn't expect me to wear "dress pants." After all, we weren't going to church. I didn't want to dress-up for anybody or anything. My jeans, a t-shirt, and tennis shoes were just fine.

Damn again, I thought. Mom said she was going to call my sister's mother. How did she know who my sister's mom was? Did mom know all along where my sister lived and who she was? Those mixed emotions came creeping in once more. How could they, my sister's parents and mine, have kept us apart for so long? There was nothing fair about being adopted, always being surprised by what was being withheld or what you had missed, searching for answers you are never sure you can find. I could by no means figure out if I was happy or sad when these moments were unveiled. I surmised being adopted was a sensation of being happy-sad.

It took awhile, but as sure as death, the moment did arrive. Mom and I loaded into the family car and drove away, leaving dad at home, heading toward our destination – a joyous reunion. We arrived in Welch in about twenty minutes and slowly made our way through town. This happened to be a payday weekend for the area coal miners. So, traffic was a bit heavy on the one-way streets crisscrossing the many sections of town.

Welch was the main shopping center for all of McDowell County, and the town's variety of shops did a booming business on the Saturday's following miners' payday. For a small town, there was about anything you could imagine for sale from the business establishments. There were department stores, men's and women's specialty stores, hardware stores, furniture and appliance stores. And two drug stores with soda fountains, served rich, thick milk shakes, tasty, greasy hamburgers, fries, and of course, a million flavors of ice cream. There was also a fancy hotel where many travelers checked-in when in town for business. Not too many people visited for tourism's sake or vacations.

The town had its social divisions just like the big cities. For example, the houses lining the residential streets nearest downtown were large colonial designed homes with several rooms and screened-in porches and inhabited by mostly lawyers, doctors, and other well paid professionals. The working class citizens lived in houses situated on the hillsides surrounding and overlooking the town on streets with names like Hobart or Little Hobart.

The majority of the people of Welch, and of McDowell County in general, were friendly and peaceful. Visitors to the area were always welcomed and greeted with a smile and handshake. But there was also an element of roughness and toughness that seems to exist in most mining towns. This segment of the population was noticeably present on payday weekends and usually put on a boxing exhibition somewhere in town before the day was over. For a small town, there were an awful lot of fights occurring in the city streets. But there was one time of year, well maybe two if you count Christmas, when the people of the county came together for celebration. On Veterans Day people made their way into town early in the morning and lined the sidewalks in joyful anticipation of marching bands from all of the county schools, hundreds of decorated floats, and members of the many civic organizations parading in the streets to recognize the many war veterans that hailed from the town and surrounding area. McDowell County was the location chosen for the first War Memorial building in the United States. The structure was erected near Welch in the 1920's in memory and honor of the brave World War I veterans. The building was also home for about a thousand pigeons that kept custodians busy cleaning-up an endless stream of bird crap. The conditions were so bad that the entire building was routinely painted a slimy green color every two years.

On the other side of town we turned onto a side street I had never been on before. We followed the street to the rear of Welch Emergency Hospital. At first, I was wondering what kind of trick might be played out this time. Instead of visiting a long-lost sister, was I really being admitted to a hospital for God knows what reason? However, the sick feeling in the pit of my stomach soon passed when mom explained we would need to park near the hospital and walk a block or so to where my sister lived. There was limited parking space near her house.

The walk was only about five or ten minutes. We stopped briefly in front of, not a house, but an apartment building. Mom opened a gate to the property. We followed a narrow concrete sidewalk along the side of the building to a door located near the center of the structure. Mom opened the door. We stepped inside onto a hardwood floor at the bottom of a steep stairway. There were over twenty steps to climb before reaching a solid wooden door at the top of the staircase where mom knocked three times.

After a few seconds, the sound of locks and latches being released came from the other side of the door. My body was tense and the palms of my hands were wet. I was so nervous I could feel my knees vibrating against each other. Suddenly, the door swung open, revealing a well dressed lady and a little girl who stood facing me. She was just an inch or so taller. She wore a colorful green flowered dress that extended below her knees, white socks and black shoes with one strap and a bow crossing over the tops of her feet. Her hair was jet black and hung the full length of her back with the front sporting evenly trimmed bangs that covered the forehead to just above her captivating dark eyes. Her complexion was smooth and tan and surrounded a beautiful smile that featured glistening white, perfectly shaped teeth. She was the prettiest girl I had ever seen. She was my sister. I was proud.

"Please come in. I am so glad you could come today," the lady said as we entered through the doorway.

After an affable introduction and as mom and the lady moved toward the sofa in the living room, my sister and I headed off to another part of the apartment to play. We had not been officially introduced as sister and brother, but we somehow knew what our roles were for the moment. We entered a small room filled with more toys than I had ever seen in any G. C. Murphy's toy store. There were a couple of chairs, a small table with a lamp, and some book shelves with several books that appeared to be well used. There was one window overlooking the back street behind the apartment where most of the tenants parked their cars and the sidewalk that mom and I had traveled from our car to the building.

Most of the toys were for girls, but there was a compact record player where we spent much of our time playing Gene Autry's recording of "Home, Home on the Range" and some Shirley Temple songs. We did a lot of jumping and laughing, but very little talking. I did ask if she knew that we were brother and sister. Her only reply was, "Yes, I know."

She served us both imaginary tea and cookies and handed me a baby doll. "It's her bedtime," she said. "Rock her to sleep." I did as she asked and thought how weird it was to be playing with a doll and a girl, even if she was my sister. I wished we could have gone outside and tossed a ball back-and-forth or rode a bike. But this baby doll thing was going to take some getting used to.

The time together passed quickly and soon it was time to leave. We raised our arms ever so slightly, gently touching hands and quietly whispering, good-bye. As mom and I reached the bottom of the stairs, we paused momentarily and looked back at the figures standing on top of the precipitous flight of steps. No words were spoken as the door closed and the latches and locks were engaged.

Our visit was so brief. We hardly got to know each other (although the brief stay did produce some revelation). My sister now had a face and a name. I wondered if she and I would ever be together again. There was the hope we might one day attend the same junior high or high school together (a hope that was destroyed when her family moved out-of-state a year after my visit). But for the moment, I loved the fact I had a sister living so close to where I lived. I also had a feeling we may never know each other with the same friendship like I had with Flick and some of my other friends.

Rebekah appeared to be most content.

SEVEN

Flick and I had bonded like brothers and had encountered an incident together that taught us a lot about loyalty and true friendship. It was an event that linked us forever as best friends. Bonding was something I really needed, but I didn't know I was lacking such a relationship. Being separated from my birth mother after bonding with her for the first two years of my life had greatly affected my self-confidence without understanding what I was experiencing emotionally.

It was mid-July and the summer days were long and hot. Flick and I had just finished an invigorating swim, diving into the river from the infamous big rock, splashing among the catfish, garbage, and turds. We didn't mind the filth, the water cooled the days.

We left the river's enticing touch and moved to the school playground to play baseball, having foregone the football passing for now. Baseball was the "in thing." Located in front of the school building, a short distance from the bus stop was a single-lane bridge. It spanned about one hundred feet over the Tug Fork River connecting the two ends of highway severed by the river's gorge. Automobile drivers approaching the bridge watched for oncoming traffic and alternated the yielding of right-of-way. At the end of the bridge nearest the school, a section of guardrail extended approximately thirty feet beyond where the bridge structure abruptly stopped. This particular section was about eight to ten feet from the edge of the paved road and was shaded by two mighty oaks creating the perfect conditions for the guardrail to act as a park bench. This is where some of the community's, shall we say, less than respectable crowd "hung-out." These indolent car-gazers gawked at passer-byes just for the sake of expressing how tough and cool they were; and, in some sort of psychotic way, thought some of the women might return their gawp with a possible sexual favor. That's what Flick and I had been told by some of the older boys who were usually present on the playground. I have to admit, the bridge gang, as they were labeled, was a malevolent-looking crew. There were guys with long, usually greasy, hair, short hair, beards, mustaches, no facial hair, muscle shirts, plain t-shirts, no shirts, boots, tennis shoes, or no shoes. Their bodies were painted with scars and plenty of tattoos. A few of them looked to be innocent teenagers with baby-smooth skin – but all of them were a bunch of low-life, lazy, good-for-nothing red neck assholes. I always wondered how and where they got the money to buy all of their stuff. The cigarettes and chewing tobacco were always present in their mouths. It made their breath so foul; and, the beer and moonshine made their language so vulgar. What a bunch of losers.

Two of the longhaired tattooed gang members began yelling to Flick and me. "Hey, you little bastards, throw the baseball to us," one of them shouted.

"Yeah, give us the ball or we will kick your little asses," the other bellowed.

"No way," Flick retorted, as we moved toward the opposite side of the school ground to get farther away from the space cadets. That's when we saw the two goons enter the schoolyard and head in our direction. Simultaneously, Flick and I began to run. The two punks were in pursuit. However, it became apparent that even though they were much older, the years of chain-smoking and drinking had taken its toll and their speed did not come close to that of two well conditioned minors. We exited the backside of the grounds onto a dirt road, glancing over our shoulders to see the galloping studs fading in the dust. That's when we heard an unfamiliar word being injected into the name-calling charades, one that had an atypical ring to it. Even at eight years of age, we had been around older kids enough to learn the meaning of several odious terms, but this word seemed to elevate the act of derision to a whole new level.

"We'll get you...you little niggers," they shrieked as their legs turned to rubber and they struggled to breathe, each one coughing and choking on dust and phlegm.

Flick and I headed for his house. We knew that something good to eat would be waiting for us. And, Flick wanted to ask his grandma what the word nigger meant. We arrived at Flick's home to find his grandma sitting in her favorite rocking chair, knitting a sweater for one of Flick's sisters. She greeted us with a smile, as she always did, and asked if we were hungry.

Flick's mom shouted from inside the house, "You boys sit down on the porch and I will bring you a peanut butter and jelly sandwich. Do you want milk with that or juice?" she asked.

"We'll take milk," we both responded.

Flick went straight to the point with his grandma, asking bluntly, "Grandma, what does the word nigger mean?"

She stopped rocking and slowly leaned forward and asked, "Where did you two hear that word?"

Flick and I joined in together to explain how we were introduced to the term. We told her every minute detail of our encounter with the thugs from the bridge.

She sat silent for a moment, and then replied with an expression on her face and a sparkle in her eye that I would later understand as the look of wisdom. "It is a word some people use out of ignorance, when the person don't know no better, to ridicule another person for no reason at all. Usually, the word nigger is directed at black people. The word really means to be very poor and dirty. Dirty, like you ain't had a bath for days, even weeks, because you don't have a place to wash. Some people are really that poor, like black people were when they was slaves. But sometimes, white people are just as poor. There are some people, like politicians, that thinks black people should still be slaves. And, some black people are still angry and bitter over slavery and think that white people owe them something because of it. But that ain't right either. Thank God in Heaven there are people both black and white that don't feel that way and they don't call each other terrible names. They don't want to live in the past. Sometimes we have to look into the past to help us see the future. But, if we try to live in the past, there ain't no future. What's done is done and ain't nothing we can do that will ever change it. But we can look to the future and try to make life better for all people regardless of the color of their skin. That's one of the good things about you boys being friends. You see each other just as you is. It don't matter about your skin color. You are just two boys that like each other and wants to have fun playing together. You make each other laugh. You are both happy doing things together. That is what life is all about, being happy. So, don't ever let those people that say nasty things come between you two and your friendship. No matter what color they may be, they are afraid of what you represent – a change from the past, hope of a new beginning. There is no sweeter sound to my ears than when I hear you two boys laugh. So, don't you two be like those others that like to poke ridicule at people. Be smarter than that and do not join in with anyone in calling someone else names. These are the best days of your lives, while you are young, spending time together as friends. Remember boys, right is always right and wrong is always wrong. And, being disrespectful to anyone is wrong."

One of the truths I learned from that discussion was that Flick and I were both being called niggers by the older white boys. But in reality, it was only directed at Flick. I think Flick realized that too. He cried. If being called such an appalling moniker hurt me so much then it had to be heart-wrenching pain for Flick. I think for the first time in our lives, we both realized that we were different colors, different races. Of course, we could see that all along, but it never mattered. It still didn't matter. We had lost some of our innocence, but we became better individuals because of it. The experience brought us closer together and we both had a deeper understanding and appreciation of each other's feelings. From that day forward, Flick and I could tell each other anything in confidence. We leaned on each other when we needed someone to listen and to care. I thought I understood exactly how Flick felt that day on the schoolyard. But really, I had no way of knowing his true feelings at that time. However, just a few short weeks later, I, too, encountered another one of life's gruesome lessons on how words can cut deeper than a two-edged sword.

My cousin, Seth, lived across the street from where I lived. He was the son of my Father's younger brother, Dustan. My cousin's grandparents, on his mother's side, lived a few houses down from his house on the same side of the street. Seth occasionally received a visit from Bret. Bret was Seth's cousin who lived in another county and was the son of the only sister of Seth's mother. Bret was an only child with no brothers or sisters.

During one of his visits, Seth and Bret were playing in my cousin's front yard; and, seeing me emerge from my house, immediately summoned me over to engage in the fun. So, I obliged and joined the two of them for some typical eight year old boy's play. It did not take long for the frolicking and laughter to bring my uncle and aunt out of their abode to investigate the sounds of thunder.

Merging from his castle, my Uncle Dusty quickly inquired, "What are you doing here?" staring at me with a penetrating glare.

"I just came over to play with the guys," I replied shyly.

"Well, you need to go home now," he commanded. "Let Seth and his cousin play together," he added.

"But, I'm his cousin, too," I said pointing in the direction of Seth.

"No you're not! You're adopted," he growled. "Get the hell out of here."

Merely the sound of his voice was enough to send chills up and down my spine and drive me off his property. Back on friendly turf, so I believed, I was alone and filled with mixed emotions. I wasn't sure how I was supposed to feel. Should I tell my mom and dad or would that get me into deeper trouble? After all, I must have done something wrong for my uncle to be so upset with my presence.

Then I began to understand. Being adopted must be bad like being a different color or maybe having a funny-looking lip. I had no idea what I was supposed to do. My cousin was not really my cousin, yet, everyone said that he was. My mom and dad were not really my mom and dad. I have sisters and a brother, but they are no longer my sisters and brother. But, we had the same birth mother and father. What in the world was true and what was make-believe? This was so messed-up. When you're adopted it must mean you're not a part of this family and your real family doesn't want you. That's the way I saw it. I now knew exactly how Flick felt about the "n" word. My uncle had just called me a nigger. I cried.

I never told anyone about the ordeal – except Flick.

Well, I did tell Spot, my dog. Spot always seemed to understand exactly how I was feeling. He licked my face and sat very close to me. Flick also understood what I was going through. It seems that after he and I had the talk with his grandmother, she had further explained to Flick that the "n" word was most often directed toward black people and over time that I, too, would come to know that. She did not believe I could ever know how hurtful the "n" word could actually be to Flick. That was, until Flick told her what my uncle had said to me.

She explained that for the first time in her life she believed that someone of the Caucasian persuasion really understood how hurtful name-calling could be. And, how alone and isolated it made the recipient of such bigotry feel. Being called names gives you a feeling of rejection, of not being accepted for who you are, being told that you are different and that being different is bad or wrong. To be perceived as an outcast is difficult to grasp. It is hard to develop trust in anyone. And, identifying or recognizing truth is even a more complex process.

Now, looking back, Flick's grandmother had given us both knowledge and compassion as two important tools to help fight the cruelty of the crude and rude word attacks. But sadly enough, no amount of preparation can ease the pain of such thoughtless remarks.

Flick and Spot remained the only two living beings I knew I could trust. Without them, I would have truly been alone. Flick and I remained inseparable friends for the next few years – until that fateful night when heartbreak crashed down on us.

EIGHT

In addition to coal, another product of McDowell County's rugged terrain and multiple hollows was and is the famous "mountain dew" or moonshine that many liked to brew and sell to those with a weakness for strong drink. Most moonshiners would tell you they got into the illegal trafficking of spirits because they were poor and in need of money. In most cases, this was probably true. However, after being in the business for a while, many just did it for the taste of good liquor and the excitement of being in defiance of the law. Such was the case of one bad-ass man known as Big John.

Big John drove a large, dark blue Cadillac, evidence that business must be pretty good. Flick and I used to see Big John driving through the community occasionally waving to the bridge gang as he passed. No doubt, the gang members were some of his regular customers. Flick said he had seen Big John at one of his neighbors, Bones, late at night. The neighbor was called Bones because he was so thin that he looked liked nothing but a stack of bones. When he had his shirt off, it was easy to count every rib in his emaciated body. Bones wasn't a bad guy. He was always joking with Flick and me, saying funny things like: hey what's up knuckleheads or hey, you two look like salt and pepper just like the hair on my head.

Bones would go out to Big John's car and sit inside, talking to Big John for several minutes. Afterwards, Bones would get out of the car, wave good-bye, and watch Big John drive away. He would then carry something concealed inside a brown paper bag to the backside of his house. Flick would watch through his bedroom window until Bones disappeared around the corner. This happened every Tuesday and Friday nights just like clockwork. Flick and I knew what was in the paper bag.

Once we overheard some adults discussing Big John. They described him as no ordinary violator of the law. He was above average intelligence and social standing, whatever that meant. He was also considered a dangerous man and it was believed he was actually the leader of a band of lawless characters that distributed moonshine over several surrounding counties. There was also the story that he had shot a deputy sheriff in the face when the officer pulled Big John over for an apparent traffic violation. Big John never went to trial for the incident because the deputy was later killed in a car accident. The charges against Big John were dropped due to lack of evidence...or so the story goes. The real reason, according to my dad, was Big John was paying the sheriff a nice sum of money each month to leave him alone and not interfere with his delivery business. Regardless of how embellished or factual any of those stories may have been, one thing was definitely true, Big John was one mean dude.

On one of Big John's visits to see Bones, he and Bones went to the backside of Bones' house instead of sitting in Big John's car. Neighbors heard them laughing and talking loudly for several minutes. No doubt, they were sampling some of the fruits and over indulged just a bit. People living next door to Bones heard what sounded like a gunshot, probably a pistol, and peered through their upstairs bedroom window to investigate. Under the ashen moonlight, they observed Big John holding a small pistol and aiming it at a target nailed to a large oak tree between

Bones and Flick's houses. One of the shots from the gun missed the intended target and entered Flick's bedroom window. Flick was looking out the window about the same time, as was his custom when Big John came to call.

Early the next morning the phone rang. Mom was already out of bed, starting to prepare breakfast. I heard mom answer the phone with, "Hello," then remain silent. Curiosity led me to the kitchen where I found mom holding the phone to her ear, listening.

"What?" she whispered. "Oh…my goodness…"

"What's wrong: What's wrong?" I asked.

Dad came in, eyes all bloodshot from the sudden awakening. He had been in bed for only a short time after coming home from working all night.

"Yes, we will," my mother was saying. "Yes, of course…as soon as we can. I am so sorry, Mrs. Williams."

Mrs. Williams was one of Flick's neighbors who would sometimes buy catfish from Flick and me after one of our successful fishing ventures. She knew my family would want to know about Flick's injuries and how it had all happened.

When mom returned the phone to its cradle, her eyes were filled with tears, and her face was as pale as a ghost. Mom looked at dad, then at me. "Flick has been shot," she said. I felt the blood rush from my head and plunge to my feet. It was hard to breathe.

Within fifteen minutes, we were on our way to the hospital in Welch. I sat in the back seat of the car, my thoughts blurred by the sad news. Flick was in emergency surgery. The damage was extremely bad, according to Mrs. Williams who had filled us in on all of the horrendous details. I swore to myself Big John would pay for this…with his life.

The hospital was a four-story building of brown brick and thick glass. It appeared rather small for a place that contained so many rooms: emergency room, operating room, patient rooms, and waiting rooms. How could so many rooms fit into such a small-looking building? We entered through the emergency room where the smell of medicine was enough to make you sick. A nurse with a cap pinned to the top of her gray hair directed us to where we should go. We found Flick's parents sitting in a waiting room decorated with a couple of pictures of angels hanging from the dull almost dirty white plaster walls. The room was filled with chairs and four end tables holding stacks of magazines that no one felt like reading. Some members of another suffering family were flipping the pages of some of the reading material stopping briefly to look at the pictures. Flick's dad was wearing a light weight jacket with blood smeared all over the front. It was a sight that took all of the air right out of me. There was blood on his face and hands too. I guess he was in too much shock to wash his face and hands in the nearby bathroom.

Mom gave Flick's mother, Almadean, a tender hug. They both began to cry. Dad spoke to Flick's dad as they stared from a window into the early morning haze. None of Flick's brothers or sisters had made the trip, probably not enough time to pull everything together. Flick's grandmother was there. No way was she going to stay behind at home.

I sat down and picked up a magazine. My eyes could not focus on any of the pages.

"How does something like this happen?" I heard Flick's dad asked. "Why?"

Mom sat next to Almadean and touched her hand softly. Occasionally, a bell would sound somewhere in the hospital's halls and a voice would come over a speaker system, "Paging Dr. Sizemore or Dr. Brae."

A minister from the Roderfield African Zion Church entered the room and approached Flick's mom. She was a member of the church and, along with Flick's grandmother, attended Sunday school and Sunday praise service every week. Flick had to go to Sunday school every Sunday and stay for church service at least two out of every four Sundays. The minister asked all of us to hold hands and bow our heads for prayer. I believed that prayer changed things. I prayed that Flick would get well and be all right. I prayed and believed with all of my heart.

Others were starting to come in, and the waiting room was soon full. Most were Flick's neighbors, but a few were people I had never seen. Maybe it was just my sadness, but I noticed that some of the people looked at mom, dad, and me as if to say, "What are you doing here?" It gave me a very uncomfortable feeling. That's when I became aware that we were the only white people in the waiting room. I suddenly felt unwelcomed and out of place. Flick's grandmother sensed the same thing. In her wisdom, she quickly proclaimed to the entire crowd that I was Flick's best friend – the best friend he had ever had or would ever have.

For a moment the whispering and dinging bells drifted into the background and faded to silence. I found myself alone with my thoughts. Just a brief time ago, Flick and I were riding bikes and playing baseball. How quickly this awful event had happened and touched so many lives. Flick had been in the operating room for over seven hours.

"He will make it. He's strong. He'll make it," I shouted, coming back to reality and the voices of concern.

By now, Mr. Johnson had discarded the jacket and washed his face and hands. He still wasn't saying much, just pacing back and forth across the room. A doctor dressed in green hospital clothing entered the room and asked to speak privately with Mr. and Mrs. Johnson. They exited the room for the hallway. No one said anything, not a word. We all just stared toward the doorway waiting anxiously for some news, some good news.

It was almost midnight when Dr. Brae and a nurse entered the waiting room, huddled with Flick's mom and dad. Mr. Johnson, after clearing his throat, told everyone that Flick was out of the operating room area and had been moved to a recovery room. His condition was still very serious and only time would tell if he could pull through. He thanked everyone for coming and being there for support. He suggested that we all go home to get some rest.

Most of the people began to leave, each one stopping momentarily to speak with Mr. and Mrs. Johnson. The minister said he would remain for as long as the family wanted him there. Mrs. Williams and her husband stayed for about a half-hour longer. Gradually, the room thinned out. Flick's grandmother grasped mom's hand and asked that we remain for a little longer. So we waited as the others slowly departed.

The windows were misty as fog drifted across making it difficult to see much of anything on the outside. Sitting for so long in such a depressed environment made you feel like you were in prison being punished for something you knew nothing about.

Dad and Mr. Johnson went for a cup of coffee dispensed from a machine down the hall. They returned a short time later and announced that Dr. Brae had sent word that Flick had come to and was now conscious. Flick's parents linked hands and rushed to Flick's side.

After about fifteen minutes, which seemed like an eternity, Mr. Johnson came back into the waiting room. Even though his skin was dark brown in color, he was as pale as a ghost. There was no sparkle of joy in his eyes, just a dull look of grief. Maybe his look of sorrow was because the visitation time in intensive care was limited to ten minutes per visit; or, maybe because only one person at a time was allowed in the room with Flick. It was the hospital rules.

But rules or not, Flick's grandmother stood up and said she was going in. Mr. Johnson stopped her and said Flick had asked for me. I was afraid.

Flick's grandmother said encouragingly, "It's all right. You go ahead. I'll be here all night with him. He needs his best friend right now."

I followed Mr. Johnson down the hall. Just outside the entrance to the intensive care unit, the minister and Dr. Brae stood talking, almost in a whisper. There was an eerie feeling as we passed. Inside Flick's room, Mrs. Johnson was sitting in a chair beside Flick's bed. There were several plastic tubes protruding from underneath the sheets and connecting to bags containing blood and other brownish colored liquids. From overhead a couple of smaller plastic tubes snaked down from bags of clear liquids and joined needles that were inserted into Flick's hands and arms and held in place with surgical tape. A machine was nearby that had a green wavy line running across its black monitor where a dot would frequently appear with a blipping sound and move from left to right on the screen. The bed was covered with a plastic oxygen tent. Trying to see through it was like trying to peer through the fogged-up windows in the waiting room.

Mrs. Johnson saw me and leaned over near the tent close to Flick's head. "He's here, Clarence."

Mrs. Johnson stood up and moved her chair near the head of the bed. "You can set here next to Flick," she said pointing to the chair.

She and Mr. Johnson went to stand near the door. I looked through the oxygen tent at my friend's face, what I could see of it. There was a tube coming out of one of his nostrils and one from the side of his mouth. His head was completely wrapped with white gauze, like a cap, that extended down one side of his face, hiding his right eye, and disappearing beneath the sheet that covered his body. With his dark smooth skin, Flick looked like Egyptian royalty, only very sick. He stared at me with a look that was distant, as if he were asleep with his eye open. His breathing was labored and heavy. I wasn't sure if he could see me or speak at all. I spoke softly to him because that seemed like the appropriate thing to do. I told him how sorry I was that this had happened and that a lot of people had come to the hospital to be with him. I explained that Reverend Emerson was there, and everyone was praying for him to get better. I told Flick the prayers would be answered. I reached under the oxygen tent and grasp Flick's hand. He gave my hand a gentle squeeze as I told him I had to leave. However, I promised to come back the next day to check on him. I said I had to go because my visiting time was up.

Flick began to slowly move his lips trying to say something. I moved closer as Flick repeated the words. "You have to go because you are adopted."

We smiled.

When you are young, you don't spend much time thinking about mortality. The only time you really think of death is when someone close to you dies. Most of the time, you get over it within a few days, and by the end of a year or so, you hardly recall the person at all. Of course, war is different. You expect death, you see death, and you feel death on a daily basis. So, one would think that because death is so common that it would be easily dismissed or soon forgotten. Not so. It works just the opposite. Each fatality touches you in a special way. It's like a part of you dies with each casualty, and there is no revivification. Flick's death was a war death – K.I.A. (killed in action). He died a hero. I know he's in Heaven.

NINE

Within sixty days after Flick's burial, the police investigation was completed, and the findings were presented to a grand jury. As predicted by many in the community, including Flick's dad, the grand jury ruled there was insufficient evidence to prove the incident was more than just an unfortunate accident and failed to return an indictment. However, the D.A. managed to get a hearing on the discharge of a weapon in a public place, causing a death. If convicted, Big John would face up to ten years for involuntary manslaughter. Big John had stated he had not been target shooting with the gun, and in fact, he had no idea the gun was loaded. Big John maintained he was simply looking at the gun as a possible purchase. It discharged as he was handing the pistol back to Bones. Again, the man's reputation preceded him, and the judge ruled that the district attorney had not proved beyond a shadow of doubt that Big John caused the gun to fire, and that the event took place on private property, not a public place, by the court's definition. He was simply reprimanded for discharging a firearm within fifty feet of an occupied residence. Since there was no official statute or ordinance to support the judge's ruling, Big John's attorney had the opportunity to appeal the court's decision. But as one might expect, he was visibly elated the imposed punishment came down to only three months probation and a one hundred dollar fine. Big John looked in the direction of Flick's family and laughed out loud. There was no appeal.

I wanted to kill the son of a bitch. I just had to figure out when, where, and how...no small task for an eleven year old boy. My effrontery convinced me that I could do it without culpability...but how and when? Then the idea struck me like a bolt of lightning. Halloween was soon approaching. Big John would be out and about in our area, I was sure. The spooks and goblins were due to make an appearance on a Tuesday night this particular year, and Big John would have a rendezvous with Bones.

On Halloween, the older boys, and some of the adults, would always block the narrow road running through our camp. It was a tradition. They would use cinder blocks, trash, wood, broken glass, or anything else they could get their hands on. Sometimes they would even use a chain saw to fell a tall tree near the edge of the road. What I wanted to know was where the location would be and the time of the upcoming annual prank? I knew it would be late, maybe after midnight, when the dastardly deed would occur. These guys needed to be convinced to do it around the time Big John arrived. Could I do the convincing?

I decided to enlist the assistance of Teddy French, a guy about the age of twenty-one or twenty-two, who occasionally hung-out with Jamal, one of Flick's older brothers. Jamal was once a light weight amateur boxer, and Teddy was his stiffest competition. After many unsuccessful attempts to defeat Jamal in area and statewide tough-man bouts, Teddy decided to throw in the towel. But to his credit, Teddy did not hang his head in shame. Instead, he became Jamal's sparring partner, which only helped to make Jamal a more skillful fighter. In fact, at the time of Flick's death, Jamal was representing the US Army in a boxing tournament in Germany. Flick's dad convinced Jamal not to come home for the funeral. He wanted Jamal to win the tourney for Flick. He thought Flick would have wanted that too. And Jamal did just that – an amazing first-round knockout of a much more experienced fighter in the championship match. The Army rewarded Jamal's dramatic outcome and sacrifice with the approval of a tribute to Flick by engraving on the base of the trophy the inscription: In memory of Clarence "Flick" Johnson – one brave soldier.

Of course, Teddy's help had to come without his knowledge he was actually doing anything on my behalf. I knew Teddy would know all of the details for any blockades whether he was participating or not. He was not one of the bridge gang regulars. However, he was more than just acquainted with some of them. He was actually a good friend with a few. After all, Teddy was not what I considered to be a bad guy, but everyone knew for certain he was no angel.

After a few evenings on the school grounds passing ball with the other boys, Teddy finally made an appearance at the bridge mob's headquarters. The meeting had the resemblance of a posse gathering for a midnight ride. They appeared to be waiting for their fearless leader, Dudley Do-Right. I watched patiently for Teddy to leave and hoped he departed alone. It was just before darkness fell when Teddy made his departure. He left alone, thank God. I said my good-byes to the guys and ran to catch-up with puppet man Teddy.

"What's up Ted," I said with caution.

"Hey, kid, what's up with you?" he replied.

"Not too much…have you heard from Jamal lately?" I asked nervously.

"Naw, haven't heard from him in quite some time. Guess he's doing OK though. You were good friends with his little brother, weren't you?" he inquired.

"Yeah, Flick was my best friend. Too bad Big John didn't get what he deserved," I said.

"That's why he's called Big. He's too big around

here. Somebody needs to take him down a notch or two, don't you think little man?" Teddy surprisingly remarked.

"You bet. Wouldn't it be great if a headless horseman paid him a visit on Halloween? Maybe he would disappear like Ichabod Crane," I added. "If someone is going to block the road this year, maybe they could wait for Big John to go by and then set the blockade while he is doing business with Bones. Then, when he gets out of the car to move the rocks or whatever, someone could bomb him with eggs or tomatoes or maybe even a rock or two," I suggested.

"That's not a bad idea, buddy," Teddy said. "You know the road is going to be blocked. That's a given. I'll see what I can do about Big-ass John. Maybe some of the others will want to see the motherfucker sweat a little bit too. Sounds like fun. Thanks for the brainstorm, kid. This whole thing adds a pinch of madness to what we do," Teddy said laughingly as he bade me farewell.

I was actually thrilled. Halloween was only a week away. But then I realized I still didn't know exactly where the road block would be or what time it would all come down. There seemed to be two logical places ideally suited for the obstruction. One was in the bend of the road at the top of the hill on the south end of the community. Here the curve was more than a ninety degree turn. It was more like a horseshoe shape bend. On one side of the road was the hillside where several available trees stood ready to be sacrificed. On the opposite side of the road was a drop-off that was approximately one-hundred feet above the railroad tracks below. There was no way for a vehicle of any type to pass a barrier at this location without first stopping and clearing a path to follow. If a tree was the obstruction, drivers would need a chain saw to cut an opening; or, wait for someone to come along who had a saw or a chain and large enough truck to drag the tree out of the roadway.

Also, the hillside provided excellent cover and location to launch a missile attack. Even if the stalled motorist initiated a quick retreat, there would not be enough time to turn the automobile around before encountering a barrage of unforgiving projectiles.

The second possible, but less likely, place was at the end of the bridge, opposite the end where the bridge gang parked their dirty butts, where the road narrowed at the bridge approach. If this happened to be the chosen location, the bridge faithful would have front row seats for the main attraction. However, since several of the mendicants were customers of Big John, and their presence would surely be noticed, it was unlikely that they would run the risk of being identified and having to endure his retaliatory wrath.

Halloween arrived right on time. The school classrooms were laden with a costume mixture of animals, outer space aliens, monsters, cartoon characters, and past presidents. The more eccentric observers exchanged cards and candy. No one hung around after school. I guess the excitement was too much, wanting to get an early start on bagging all that colorfully wrapped cavity-making tooth decay. My mind was not on candy, but on the sweetness of seeing Big John bite the big one. The plan was to go out as usual and do the trick-or-treat scene with my cousin, Seth, and a few other neighborhood kids. We planned to soap the Thompson's windows and of course, sling a bag of flaming shit onto the porch of the Henderson's. And naturally, we would collect our share of the chocolate bullion before returning home by the nine o'clock curfew. After that, the real plan would go into motion.

I was in bed by ten with the door to my room shut, the lights out, and the window open. Mom retired shortly after ten, and dad was at work for the night. I was free to execute my plan – and Big John. I dressed in jeans, a black sweatshirt, black brogan shoes, and a dark brown toboggan, grabbed my Mickey Mantle autographed Louisville Slugger, and climbed through the window.

I made my way to the sharp curve by moving quickly and quietly through several neighborhood yards, then along an upper level dirt road, avoiding the main road, afraid of being recognized if seen by some passing motorist. On arrival, I was pleasantly surprised to see a tree had been downed and lay motionless across the darkened highway. Without hesitation, I positioned myself in the brush off to the side of the road where I could easily observe any activity near the tree. I was so nervous, I had to piss.

I was puzzled by the baleful silence surrounding me. Where was everybody? Surely someone besides me had planned to watch the mayhem about to be unleashed on some poor soul, hopefully, Big John. Maybe the tree had been cut too soon or too late. If Big John was not going to be in the picture, then why stick around. After all, the tradition was in tact. That had to be it. Big John had probably changed his modus operandi for the evening and thus avoided all the fun. Crap, I had taken a chance of a lifetime for nothing...nothing except a possible beating for sneaking out of the house without permission. Then it dawned on me. How was I going to rush out of my hiding place, conk Big John over the head with a baseball bat, roll his blubbery body over the edge of the drop off, and get away without being seen? If there were bushwhackers hiding somewhere nearby, I would be crazy to follow through with my act. I'd be caught in a New York minute. Oh well, maybe all of this was for naught anyway. It had to be divine intervention, although I couldn't understand how God could or would intervene for someone like Big John.

I was just about to pack it in and call it a night when the appearance of car lights hit the slumbering tree stretched out across the pavement. I crouched down and settled in to watch the imminent clamor of activity that awaited the approaching person or persons, assuming they wanted to continue their journey.

The car began to slow and then came to a complete stop. The driver opened the door and got out of the car slowly. The image stood silently next to the auto behind the glow of lights. The figure was alone, I guessed, because no one was speaking and no one else emerged from the car. I was anticipating the bombardment to begin at any moment, if there were some pranksters nearby. Nothing happened, confirming my earlier feeling that I was alone...until now. What had been a silhouette unexpectedly stepped from the darkness and into the light, revealing his personage. I could not believe what I was seeing. It was Big John all by his lonesome. But where was Teddy or some of the other guys who had blocked the road in the first place? My adrenaline began to swell. This was my break to do what I had set out to do. I was frightened, but I had to do it. I had to do it for Flick. My breathing became labored, and the taste of bile filled my mouth. Momentarily, I relaxed as the sight of a second set of lights approached. Big John moved back into the shadows as the other vehicle came to a halt.

A door opened. Big John exclaimed, "What the hell...?"

A gunshot sounded, then another. Big John staggered from the dimness to the light, clutching his chest, stumbling to the edge of the steep embankment, then falling head first over the edge, plunging to a sure death on the rails and gravel below. I quickly lay flat on my stomach, burying my face into my hands, as the night became gloom.

The violent death of Big John came as a surprise to some. But, to most, his demise was welcomed news. More moonshiners could now openly sell their brews with Big Boy gone, and there were plenty of customers looking for a supply source.

Hard to believe that was eight years ago. Now, I'm sitting here, in the bush, still wondering who pulled the trigger on Big John. I never said a word to any living soul about where I was or what I witnessed that Halloween, not even Spot. My dog was the only living creature that saw me leave my house and return that night, and he never betrayed me. The state police investigation ended with no arrests. The bullets recovered from Big John's body could not be matched to any Winchester 30-30 rifle in the area. Everyone that might have been considered a suspect had an iron clad alibi. And yet, I was there, and I don't have a clue regarding the assassin's identity. I know it wasn't Flick's dad. He was in Georgia visiting family that night. And, it wasn't Teddy. Teddy and his girlfriend were at the Star Land outdoor theater watching some double feature from the back seat of his supped-up '57 Chevy. The police never considered Teddy a suspect anyway. The one thing I do remember changing after that Halloween night was the attitude toward me by one of the assholes at the bridge. It was one of the ruffians that had chased Flick and me, calling us names, and wanting our baseball. Not with the nasty snarls as before, but when he saw me on the school grounds he would look my way and casually give me a thumbs-up sign, or simply smile and wink and say something like, "how ya doing, Kid?"

I never answered him, but, I think, in his own way, he was letting me know he had repented. And, I forgave him.

TEN

Alone, I can be anxious about some things; yet, not afraid of anything. A Marine's indoctrination I guess. But where does this audaciousness originate? Is it inherited, learned through experiences, or is courage the corollary of a great effort to survive adverse circumstances, hardening, numbing the nerves with each successive trial? Hell, I don't know. It was just a gedanken (thought). There was yet another event that happened when I was twelve years old that required a measure of bravery by a young boy facing the unknown. After all, I somehow managed to pull through the loss of Flick. Therefore, I could handle anything; or, so I thought.

My grandmother lived alone for the most part in a large house of about twenty rooms. The upstairs section was accessible from two directions: a steep, narrow stairway from the downstairs kitchen; and, from the stairway just inside the front entrance to the house. Attached to the fascia of the house was a large screened-in porch. The dimensions were approximately thirty feet by thirty feet. To access the front doorway for entry into the house, one must first cross the porch area diagonally. Once inside, the stairs were to the right and joined the foyer to an upstairs, long and narrow, hallway. The five twenty-five watt bulbs lighting the passageway emitted just enough light to guide a child's imagination through horror scenes like those found in science fiction novels.

From time to time grandmother would rent the upstairs rooms on a weekly basis for extra income and to some degree, companionship. Many of the boarders were repeat occupants. They found the accommodations comfortable and the rates reasonable.

One year, I believe it was in October of 1961, grandmother decided to spend the winter months in Florida with relatives to escape the cold and wet West Virginia climate that could send a chill to the bone of even a seasoned native of some eighty years. Always thinking of her denizens, she asked my family to temporarily abandon their abode and become caretakers at the Virginia Avenue residence. The digs were close to dad's and mom's work locations, which would save both time and money. So, the invitation was accepted.

The transition occurred early in the month, and by the end of October, all but one of the tenants had departed to their homes for the upcoming holiday season with plans not to return until the New Year. The one remaining resident, a lady, Elizabeth, did not plan to leave until the long Thanksgiving weekend.

Elizabeth often watched TV with us in the evenings, a much better option than sitting alone in her upstairs sleeping quarters listening to the radio. One evening while my mother, Elizabeth, and I viewed an episode of the "I Love Lucy Show," the telephone began to ring. Mother picked up the phone and said, "Hello," then, strangely repeated the word a second and third time.

"Probably a wrong number," she said as the telephone headset was placed back on its stand. Nothing unusual about someone dialing an incorrect number, mom and dad had made the same mistake more than once. But suddenly, the phone began to ring again.

"Hello, hello. Who's there?" mom asked firmly. No reply. Dead silence. If this was some kind of a prank call, it was not being well received. People of that day did not appreciate practical jokes, especially those employing the use of a telephone where the identity of the prankster could remain a mystery.

"Maybe that was your dad trying to reach us," mom pondered aloud while looking directly at me. She quickly placed a call to dad at his work location. Dad worked as a night watchman and night mechanic for the County Board Of Education at the county's central bus garage. He often volunteered to work over if the workload demanded it. Tomorrow was going to be one of those days. We could always use the extra money.

"Hi, did you just try to call us?" she asked as dad apparently answered the phone after only one or two rings. "You didn't? Well, someone just called twice and did not respond when I answered the phone. They're probably having a difficult time dialing the right number. Just wanted to check with you to make sure everything was okay," she explained with noticeable relief in her voice. We continued to watch Lucy with some anticipation of another ring. Thankfully, the engaging comedies of Lucy soon let us forget the brief anxiety attributable to an unknown caller.

At the end of the "I Love Lucy Show" Elizabeth retired to her room for the night. She was obviously cautious on her ascent up the flight of steps, pausing occasionally to continue a dialogue with mom, who remained positioned at the bottom of the staircase. Funny how telephone calls, with no conversation, can change the behavior of reasonable thinking adults.

"Hope the phone doesn't ring anymore tonight," she said, her voice conspicuously quivering as she entered her room and closed the door behind her.

I heard the dead bolt slide into place as mom gently shut the door to the stairs and locked it as well. "Me too," mom whispered as she pointed toward my room, a sure sign that we were all hitting the sack for the night. Even so, it was almost 9:30 PM. There was work and, of course, school to attend the next day, although a boy could use a Friday off once in awhile. But, moms don't seem to share that view. They see it as just one more day before the weekend. Surely, a child that's about to turn thirteen can make it through just one more day. In my case, I had to agree. Who wanted to stay in such a large house all by yourself for a whole day? What if the phone began to ring?

The dawning of a new day brings with it new challenges and new adventures. The events of the night before were all but forgotten. While getting dressed for school, I heard mom and Elizabeth talking in the kitchen. Mother was preparing breakfast for herself and me. Elizabeth was explaining her change in plans for going home for the holidays. She had originally planned to leave next week, over Thanksgiving, but sometime during the night, she had a change of heart and decided to leave early, like the others, and not return until the second week of January. Now it would only be our family left in the big house until after the holidays. Mom and I would spend the nights alone while dad continued to work with plans to be off only on Christmas Day and New Years Day.

School was uneventful that day with everyone looking forward to next week's three days of classes and then the long, well deserved, Thanksgiving weekend. Mom and I arrived home at about the same time. She quickly prepared the evening meal before dad left for his all night assignment. He had just gotten out of bed from what was a brief rest after working over from the previous shift. When the meal was finished, the dishes were stacked in the kitchen sink for washing. Thank God, this was a chore that could wait until morning. It was the weekend you know. Besides, if I played my cards right, by tomorrow morning mom would not remember she had asked me to do the dishes.

Dad was punctual in leaving while mom and I withdrew to the TV room for a deluge of sit-coms following the nightly network newscasts. The transmutation from twilight to nightfall was now complete, and the rush hour traffic slowed to an occasional unobtrusive passer-by.

As the miniature silver screen programming got underway, the telephone's vociferous ringing unexpectedly interrupted our viewing. Mom hurriedly picked up the receiver to answer. She did not utter a word. Somehow she knew. The mysterious caller had struck again.

"Let's not jump to conclusions," mom exclaimed as she dialed dad's work number. "It just happened again, a call with no one saying a word on the other end."

"Don't get so worked up over a phone call with no one saying anything. It's probably just some kids trying to have what they call fun. If it bothers you so much, leave the phone off the hook," dad suggested. Seemed like good advice to me as mother reiterated dad's words.

"Guess you're right. We are being somewhat silly, aren't we?" she surmised.

That's true, I thought. Why were these calls so alarming? Were they some portent of events to come?

"Sorry, we won't disturb you anymore with such nonsense. Have a good night, and we will see you in the morning." With that adieu, I knew mom would not dare call dad again, even if the ruse calls continued all night.

The phone had no more been hung-up when it began to ring one more time. Mom calmly answered with the familiar "hello" with the same results. No reply. Mother became belligerent with the caller.

"Who are you? What do you want? I have had about enough of your practical jokes. Why don't you answer?

Does the cat have your tongue?" mom impudently asked. The caller abruptly severed the connection.

About two hours of Hollywood entertainment, popcorn, and coke passed without incident. Neither of us so much as mentioned the silent phone. It looked like mom's outburst had frightened the caller into choosing some other recipient for his or her larks.

"What was that? Did you hear that?" I asked.

"Yes, I did," mom breathed. The sound of footsteps being carefully placed, softly, on the old wooden flooring of the upstairs hallway sent a chill over my entire body. As hard as one may try, there was no way to keep the wood strips from crying out when pressed down under the weight of someone's feet.

"Maybe its Elizabeth returning for some of her things, something she may have forgotten to pack. It must be Elizabeth. The only entrance to the upstairs that is out of our sight is the front doorway, but it is locked. Only someone with a key could enter without our knowing it. That could only be Elizabeth," mom hypothesized.

But why would Elizabeth return without stopping by to let us know she was there? With the sudden decision to leave early for the holidays, I hardly thought she would return and go directly upstairs on her own. She seemed too troubled by the first round of disconcerting calls.

"Be very still and quietly follow me into the kitchen," mom instructed. We slowly approached the stairwell leading from the kitchen to the upstairs. We saw that the dead bolt was secure and that no one could have entered or exited through this location without alerting us to their presence. We stood near the locked door and listened intently. Not a sound. Mom reached for the lock on the stairway door, and then guardedly unlatched the security device. She gripped the doorknob firmly and began to gradually open the door. As our hearts raced with anxiety, the door was fully opened, exposing the other side.

Thank God, no one was standing there. Mom leaned in and called out, "Is that you, Elizabeth?" No riposte. Once more, "Is that you, Elizabeth? Is there anyone there?" Again, there was not a sound. The door was quickly returned to its locked position, and we looked at each other as if to say, "Now what do we do?"

The flooring squeaked yet again. Footsteps moved down the hallway, in the direction of the staircase leading to the kitchen. Toward the same doorway that had just been opened and then closed. We could only listen, afraid to move a muscle. Reaching the top of the stairs, the footsteps paused.

"Go to the telephone and call the police," mom commanded.

Like a well-trained Marine, the orders were followed without question. "Hello, operator, please get me the police. This is an emergency," I stated, remembering how this was supposed to be done from watching hundreds of episodes of "Dragnet" on television.

"Police department, may I help you?" the calm voice asked.

"Please come quickly to 123 Virginia Ave. There is an intruder in the house," I nervously shouted. "Yes, Ms. D's house, that's correct."

The police were especially responsive to any request emanating from grandmother's address. My grandfather, one of their own, was killed in the line of duty back in the mid-1920s. He had come to the coalfields of West Virginia at a time when violence was common between the coalminers and the security guards for the coal company owners. He was considered a government agent, a G-man, sent to observe the evolution of the unions in the coal mining industry. His dedication to his work soon won the admiration of all law enforcement personnel in the surrounding area. He became active in the various police agencies, solving numerous crimes that later spawned a legendary reputation as the "boogieman" for his supernatural ability to nab villains before they could escape. The Semper Fi-like bond of this fraternal organization had been extended to a fallen brother's widow for many years. The police were always loyal to my grandmother.

"We are on our way, son," the voice proclaimed. Each second, every tick of the grandfather clock was counted until their arrival. Three hundred and thirty ticks brought a knock at the front door that echoed throughout the whole house.

"They're here, it's the police," mom said with relief. She had been observing the front door from a room that led to the foyer and was between the foyer and kitchen where the only other access to the upstairs was situated. Mom had engaged the safety chain lock and had opened the door of the room slightly. From this vantage point she watched both the front door and the stairs, just in case someone attempted to exit before the police arrived. If someone had come down those stairs, both of us would have needed a change of clothes in addition to possible heart transplants.

"We sure are glad to see you," mother joyfully beamed. "Come in. No one has come down either set of stairs. We have been closely watching."

"Report said that you have an intruder. You think someone is upstairs?" the officer inquired.

"Yes, I'm sure of it," affirmed mom thinking she had already made that clear.

"Okay. Have you seen anyone up in that area?" asked the officer.

"We have not actually seen anyone, but we did hear footsteps several times. They were coming from the hallway. I called out for identification, but no one responded. So, we called you," mother explained.

"Don't worry; we will take care of whoever is up there. You folks please stay in that room with the doors closed and locked until we finish checking the upstairs. Oh, by the way, I am Lieutenant Panetta and this is Sergeant O'Brien. There is an officer stationed outside and an officer at the back door. Could one of you unlock the door for him?" Lt. Panetta asked.

"I will," I said volunteering. That's the same statement I made at the Armed Forces Induction Center when all of us being drafted for military service were asked if we would like to volunteer. Volunteers for the two-year stint would be considered enlisted instead of drafted and stood a slim chance of avoiding Vietnam. So, I stepped forward along with several other imperceptive, I mean, brave men to accept the invitation in hopes of getting some of that "slim chance." That's how I ended up a Marine. Seems the Marines were a little short of their quota that day and all volunteers were being assigned to the Corps. Well, that's not exactly the way it was. It's sort of like being adopted. How things or circumstances seem to be, sometimes are not how they really are. Nevertheless, that's how I remember it.

"Thanks," the officer said as he entered through the back door. "Close the door and make sure it is locked." The officer went to the bottom of the stairs located in the kitchen, unlocked the door and opened it.

Lt. Panetta could see the officer positioned at the kitchen steps. "That's Sergeant Stone," he said as he gave the signal to proceed up the stairs. Officer O'Brien remained in the foyer as Lt. Panetta began the climb of the front stairs. Mother and I closed and locked the two doors of the room sealing us inside until the search was completed per the instructions from Lt. Panetta.

Once the two men were at the top of the stairs, facing each other from opposite ends of the hallway, Lt. Panetta joined officer Stone at the top of the stairs leading from the kitchen area. They worked their search room by room from one end of the hall to the other. While I was away opening the back door for Sgt. Stone, mom gave Lt. Panetta a set of keys including a master key to use to open any of the doors that may be locked. We were able to follow their progress over the hallway by listening to their footsteps on the old wooden floor. If someone was encountered and tried to escape, they had to face Officer O'Brien on their way out through the front entrance. If someone was brave or stupid enough to go through a second story window and survive the jump, Officer Bailey was outside to give the leaper an enthusiastic, jovial welcome upon landing.

The search proceeded slowly and meticulously from room to room. When each room had been thoroughly inspected, Lt. Panetta summoned mom to the upstairs. Naturally, I was close behind.

"Madame, we have checked every nook and cranny up here and found no sign of anyone being present. All of the rooms are empty. All windows are closed and locked. No way anyone could have gone out through a window and then locked it. Are there any hidden areas such as a secret passageway or even a small room that someone other than family might know about?" the Lieutenant asked.

"No hidden areas anywhere in the house," mom explained. "Did you check the attic?" mom asked, pointing to the door that concealed the stairs leading to the loft.

"No we haven't. The door was locked from this side with a dead bolt latch that would prevent entry without first unlocking the door. But, we will check it out right now. Stranger things have happened and we would not want to leave without searching that area as well," Lt. Panetta replied.

Mom retrieved the keys from the Lieutenant and quickly selected the key to match the attic door's inherent lock that was also engaged along with the dead bolt. She politely unlocked the door and simultaneously disengaged the dead bolt. With the door now open and the lights on, the two officers made their way up the flight of stairs. After only a couple of minutes, they returned with the same results to report.

"No sign of anyone being up there recently," the Lieutenant stated.

"I know you probably think we are crazy. But I know we heard footsteps in the hallway. There's no mistaking that sound with the old wooden floor being so revealing," mom said halfway embarrassed.

"That's okay. We are happy to be of service and it's good that no one is actually here. We could have had some real trouble if someone had been found. It was probably just the old floor adjusting to the temperature and not having any traffic on it for a period of time. I'm sure everything will be fine now," the Lieutenant rationalized.

Mom again thanked the officers as they left the premises. She appeared relieved the search had not turned up any trespassers. After all, the sounds were probably as the lieutenant had said, "...just the old house adjusting to temperature change and lack of traffic over the floor's surface." Old houses, especially large ones with many rooms, have or eventually develop a certain personality. They almost come alive with the spirits of all of its visitors over the years and all of the secrets they hold. Maybe it was just an exaggeration on our part. But, in my heart, I knew that the sounds we heard were real and not imagined.

One thing that still puzzled me was the sudden departure of Elizabeth. Had she heard the same footsteps that we heard or seen something that she could not explain?

One of the unlocked rooms that had been searched was Elizabeth's. All of her clothing and personal affects were gone. She had taken every one of her possessions with her when she left. I think it became apparent to mom at that moment that we may never again see or hear from Elizabeth.

Mom and I returned to the inner circle of the house, locking the doors behind us, assuring our safety inside the familiar rooms. At first we didn't speak, obviously afraid to express what our feelings were really telling us.

Mom was first to break the silence. "Want some cookies and milk before going to bed?" she asked.

"You bet," I replied. I wasn't about to go to sleep yet. I needed further assurance that whoever or whatever had been walking around upstairs was actually gone. A few minutes of silence from the upper chamber would go a long way to convince me the prowler was gone.

After the snack, we agreed it was time to get some rest. It was quite late and morning would soon arrive. Thank goodness tomorrow was Saturday and we could sleep-in. Dad would be home soon and after a small breakfast he too would retire for some much needed slumber. Mom and I retreated to our individual rooms and beds. I extinguished the lamp beside my bed and took refuge beneath the soft covers, relaxing in the silence of the moment. The darkness of the night was diminished by the brightness of a full moon peeking through the bedroom windows. Calm had settled upon me, and I once again felt safe and secure. Soon I was asleep.

Suddenly, I was awakened by mom's voice. "Wake up," she whispered. Fear griped my body. I was afraid to move. "Be quiet and come with me," mom commanded. We walked swiftly and quietly to her room where both stairways could be observed if necessary. Mom held a flashlight in one hand and a revolver in the other. I knew the time had come when mom was going to handle the situation in her own way.

The footsteps had returned. Each stride was distinct as the approach was made one step at a time down the stairs toward the kitchen doorway. Then, just short of the door, the footsteps paused. Without hesitation, mom seized the moment to make known her intentions.

"I don't know who or what you are, but I have a gun, and I am not afraid to use it," she warned. "I am going to count to three, and then I'm going to start shooting. Do I make myself clear?" There was no response.

"One," she started.

After she shouted two, the sound of footsteps was heard hurriedly going back up the stairs. And, just as before, when the footsteps reached the top of the stairs, there was silence.

Luckily, mom did not have to fire the revolver. The police were not called. Together we sat in mom's bedroom until dad arrived home from work. Mom began to explain to dad what had taken place during the night. It was now daybreak, and the sun was rising. I fell asleep as they talked.

A couple of weeks passed, and the consumption of turkey with all of the trimmings had been forgotten. Everyone's focus was now on Christmas, not much time to think about anything else, making a list and checking it twice, again and again. The mail arrived on time that second Friday in December. Along with a few ad bulletins and a billing statement or two, there was an ominous looking envelope addressed in unfamiliar handwriting to occupant with a postmark from somewhere in New Jersey. There was no return address. Mom slowly opened the packet while thinking out loud, pondering its contents. Inside was a clipping that had been removed from an unknown newspaper. She read the piece silently at first.

Then realizing the need to give me some enlightenment, she explained that the article indicated that the body of a female had been discovered in a car in a remote area about a mile from the interstate highway near Trenton, New Jersey. The car was spotted in a drainage ditch by a jogger early Thanksgiving morning. The victim had been badly beaten. The woman's hands had been tied to the steering wheel with duct tape. Her eyes were sealed shut with black and blue bruises, her face and body swollen, and knotted around her throat was a nylon rope about eighteen inches long, pulled so tightly that the flesh had split open. Her malformed condition was from an apparent savage beating and not from a car accident. No identification had yet been made, but in the margin of the page was scribbled in blue ink, the name Elizabeth. The news item ended with: there are no suspects in the case. To our knowledge, Elizabeth did not have any enemies. She did have relatives that lived in New Jersey, or so she said; but, she didn't talk much about her family.

Shortly after New Year's Day, several of the former tenants returned, and life resumed a somewhat normal pace. Grandma arrived in the spring and was welcomed with open arms. Communicating any information about the mysterious events had been purposely withheld until her return. Mom was sure that any revelation regarding Elizabeth would shock grandma to the point of a possible heart attack. Because Elizabeth's death was so tragic, mom wanted to gently break the news to her.

Grandma listened closely to every word. She sighed and then, with a look of bewilderment, inquired, "Who is Elizabeth? I have never had a tenant by that name."

Prior to reaching the age of seven or maybe eight, I remember believing, truly believing, in the existence of Santa Claus. I don't mean the so called "spirit of Santa," but Santa as a real person with flesh and bone. Then one day, out of the blue, some kid blurted out those heart-breaking words that we all wish would never come, "Santa ain't real. He's make-believe, dumb ass." I will never forget the forlorn disappointment and despair at that moment of revelation that overshadowed all of the past good memories of Christmas. Mom and dad failed to confirm the truth about make-believe when confronted with the question, "Is Santa Claus real, or not?" They didn't give me a straight answer. They continued to play the game by responding, "What do you think? Do you believe he's real?" I never answered.

So then, who was Elizabeth? Did she ever exist? I wasn't all that sure about Santa, but the person that had lived in the same house, if only for a short time, with me sure was real. There was absolutely no doubt in my mind. She had flesh and bone and spoke with a voice that was definitely human. She was not an apparition or a figment of my (or mom's) imagination. She was a bona fide human being. It is still a mystery to me why no one questioned grandma's puzzling response. No one commented at all. It was as if some hole in the world had been filled, and all was well once again. Elizabeth was forgotten.

I wondered then and even now how the people in my life, before my abduction by the state, spoke of our (my siblings and me) existence after we were taken. Were we like Santa, or were we like Elizabeth, dismissed as if we were never born? Did anyone question what had happened or why we had disappeared? Did anyone really care? Were we simply forgotten?

ELEVEN

Life with my friends in the community was a lot different than that of the routine followed at school. The pals from school lived in other neighborhoods, some located in the opposite direction from Welch, as far as twenty miles from Big Sandy. All of us kids loved to go to the ball diamond to play baseball or football depending on what sport was in season at the time. The ball diamond, as we called it, was simply a large level plot of land owned by the Norfolk and Western Railroad Company located about two miles from the neighborhood and situated near the railroad tracks. The rail company did not maintain the land, so the kids from not only Big Sandy, but also other nearby towns, adopted the field as a place for their recreation and pastime. To get to the ball field from my house, a shortcut was taken by following the railroad tracks, which cut the traveling distance by almost a mile. However, this route required us to cross a trestle or railroad bridge that was nearly three hundred feet in length, and at its highest point was over one hundred twenty feet above the Tug Fork River flowing underneath the structure. The trestle was supported by a frame of wood and iron that crisscrossed from top to bottom in a maze of x-shaped designs resting on huge concrete pilings located on the banks (both sides) of the river. The details of the construction looked much like a tall roller coaster structure at some amusement park. The older boys from our community would sometimes climb the structure from top to bottom, then back to the top. No one ever fell while performing this dangerous and stupid act that I'm aware of, but during the building of the bridge two of the workers did fall to their deaths when a supporting cable on their scaffolding platform snapped. No one ever talked about that. Norfolk and Western demolished the trestle when I was a senior in high school. It took twelve full months to rebuild the trestle with all steel frames the following year.

I remember the first time we crossed the old trestle. Hubert, Raymond, Buddy, and I had decided we were finally old enough and brave enough to take the shortcut along the tracks instead of following the longer highway route. We walked along the tracks carrying our baseball gloves, bats, and a couple of baseballs and a canteen of water. It was the middle of May, and the spring rains that forced all of the small streams and the Tug Fork to overflow their banks had finally stopped. The baseball season had gotten underway, and the thought of another exciting pennant race between the Yankees, Red Sox, and Tigers was too much for young boys to contain. We were all anxious to get into the swing of things.

We did not mention the trestle as we approached. The sound of the river rapids flowing over an underwater rocky terrain beneath the trestle added to our anxiety as the long, narrow stretch of rails spanning the deep gorge appeared before us. We stopped just short of the structure. No longer could we restrain our doubts and fears about what we were about to attempt. This was no small ordeal.

"Let's walk around," Hubert remarked.

"That would take too long," Raymond replied.

"I think a train is coming," I said. We all paused and listened. Not a sound except the river.

"Let's go. We have time to cross. There's no train coming," Raymond chimed.

"Yeah, let's get going. If we stand here long enough, a train is bound to come, you dumb asses," Buddy lamented.

"Don't start that name-calling shit, or we'll throw your ass over the edge," I added.

Buddy gave me and the others one of those looks and started walking toward the trestle, pausing momentarily and glancing back in irritation. "Are you all coming or not?"

With much uneasiness, the rest of us moved quickly to catch-up with Buddy. At first, each step was taken with caution. The fear of trying to out run a train was soon replaced with the fear of falling. The height above the river looked more like a thousand feet than a hundred. The space between the rails seemed to grow narrower as we looked across the long stretch of railroad ties that lay ahead. Our slow careful steps soon became a faster pace, and then we all started to run as we became accustomed to the spacing of the ties. Finally, we reached the other side. It had taken only three or four minutes to cross, but it had seemed more like an hour. I was sure that if a train had approached, all of us would have been killed, either by the train, the fall to the river, or the fear of both. That summer we must have crossed that old trestle more than a hundred times and only once encountered a train. Lucky for us, the train was halfway across the bridge when we arrived.

The following spring brought a newcomer to our neighborhood. Roy Smith moved from Ironton, Ohio when school was out in May. His father was a coal miner, actually a superintendent, and had been transferred by U.S. Steel Corporation to the Gary, West Virginia operations. Roy loved to play baseball.

It was the first of June when Roy made his first trip with us to the ball field. We told him about the shortcut across the trestle, and he seemed ready to make the journey.

It was early, around 8:30 in the morning, much earlier than when we usually started. There were several more boys from the community on this trip than when I made my first crossing. One of the guys tagging along this time was Nathan, a mentally challenged kid who was so much into the game of baseball that he had to sleep with his glove at night. Nathan had trouble hitting and running the bases, but he could pitch. Boy, could he pitch. He would imitate the pitchers he saw on TV right down to the spitting and the scratching. His pitches were fairly accurate with good speed. His fielding was suspect, but his reflexes were keen enough for him to protect himself from a come backer to the mound. We all watched after Nathan. He was something special.

We approached the daunting structure and stopped short in the same spot where we paused the summer before on our maiden voyage. "Well, what do you think?" I asked while watching for some expression from Roy.

"Piece of...cake," Roy replied with a touch of hesitation in his voice.

"Okay, let's go," someone shouted. We all moved forward, some singing, some whistling, and some spitting tobacco juice over the edge and watching it fall, breaking apart and disappearing before it could make it to the water below.

Buddy and I took up the rear of the pack. Roy was just in front of us, and like us on our first crossing, was extremely cautious in placing one foot in front of the other.

"I thought it was a piece of cake," Buddy said.

"What are you implying? That I'm scared?" Roy retorted.

"No, I'm saying that you are petrified, you pussy," barked Buddy.

"Bullshit, I'm not afraid of this or you," Roy said, stopping in his tracks.

Then the unthinkable…a train whistle sounded in the distance, and the tracks began to vibrate. We weren't even halfway across when the train came into view.

"Oh shit. We're all going to die," Roy panted.

"Shut the fuck up, and start running. We'll make it," Buddy yelled.

The horn blew. Everyone ran…everyone except Roy. He froze. Buddy moved quickly to Nathan and took his hand to steady his stride. I grabbed Roy by the arm and pulled him forward.

"I'm jumping," Roy said.

"Are you crazy? The fall will kill you."

The whistle blew again. Roy finally came to his senses and began to run. The train was starting to cross the trestle and closing fast. Some of the boys had reached the other side. Buddy and Nathan were only a few yards from the end. Roy and I had just passed the halfway point.

"Speed-up damn it, or we won't make it," I warned.

"Okay, okay!" Roy cried out. The train was less than fifty yards away and we still had twenty-five yards to cover. It was going to be close.

We kept running. The train was on top of us. The trestle shook. The horn blew one more time, the headlight glaring. The rest of the guys shouted to us to run faster or jump. We both jumped from the center of the tracks to the outside edge of the ties, and then leaped over the side. We fell about ten feet and landed on the embankment as the train raced past. If we had waited only one second more, we would have been splattered all over the front of that iron horse.

Our hearts pounded, and our knees were like soft rubber. We all watched as the train exited the trestle and disappeared around the bend. Roy leaned over and puked his guts out. It was a good thing he did, or I believe Buddy would have beaten the shit out of him.

We all stood for a minute trying to regain our composure when Nathan asked, "Are we going to play some ball or what?"

We started walking toward the field. Roy glanced back one more time at the trestle. Then, he spun around and hurried to the front of the group, turning his thoughts to the ball diamond and a full day of fun.

TWELVE

It was the first of October. The mountain foliage was in full transformation from green shaded hillsides to a kaleidoscope of colors still on the trees and covering the ground beneath their massive branches, exposing a sign of barrenness that would soon follow with the approaching winter. At this time of year, the thing that occupied the minds of most boys our age was sports. Oh, once in a while a girl would catch our eye and attention…but only on week days. The weekends were for focusing on more important things. The World Series was a hot topic of discussion (the Yankees of course were once again the favorites over any National League team that was yet to be determined), and the football season was in full swing with high school games every Friday night and a televised college game on Saturday afternoons. It was a great time to be a kid, especially when your team won.

The school bus pulled into its regular stop. The community kids exited down the three steps and onto hallowed ground. It was Friday. The long, arduous school week had finally come to an end. Our high school football team had an open week and would not be playing. However, all was not lost. The Saturday college football game of the week would still be televised, but none of us really gave a shit because there was another very important game to get ready for on this particular weekend – a baseball game between Big Sandy and Davy. The boys from these two neighborhoods were not the best of friends and always enjoyed the thrill of competing against one another. This game had all the flavor of a local World Series game (game seven of course) with the victor claiming supremacy until the next game or fight, whichever came first, the chicken or the egg.

Several of the guys decided to meet on the school ground, after going home and changing clothes, to pass some ball and to talk about the next day's game. There was Hubert, Buddy, Raymond, Howard, Kenneth, Roy, me, and of course, Nathan. Bill Vargis and his brother Melvin were no shows, but we knew they would not be late for the game. The Vargis' had lived in Davy at one time and were always eager to play against their old friends (and foes) as often as they could. All of us also agreed to meet early Saturday morning on the school grounds and then head to the ball field together to get in a little more batting practice just before the game. Our moms planned to pack us a cooler with sandwiches and drinks, with Howard's mom planning to drop off the goodies about a half hour before game-time. We would be set for the day. Roy announced that he had a dental appointment in Welch on Saturday morning and could not accompany us to the ball diamond that morning for batting practice. However, his mother promised to have him home in plenty of time for the game. When it was finally too dark to see the ball, we called it a night and headed home, excited about the upcoming event on Saturday.

Dawn finally arrived after a long night of tossing and turning in bed, too energized to go to sleep. Every time I closed my eyes, all I saw was the baseball bat swinging, connecting with the ball, and sending it over the right field fence (actually a row of hedges that stood about six feet tall). At some point, without realizing it, I drifted off to sleep. Now I was awake. The sun crawled through the window by squeezing through the slender opening that ran the length of the window shade from the top of the window to the window seal next to my bed. The bright rays settled upon my eyes with a warm gentle touch that rekindled the anticipation from the night before – all over again. I quickly got out of bed, dressed, and hurried into the kitchen to inhale some breakfast, told mom what kind of sandwich and drinks to have ready for Howard's mom to pickup, and then headed to the schoolyard to meet-up with the guys. A couple of the boys decided to ride their bikes to the ball field while the rest of us followed the usual shortcut that took us across the railway trestle and in the back way to the diamond. We arrived at the field about the same time and immediately started the warm-ups of tossing ball, fielding some grounders, and taking our turn swinging at Nathan's fastballs and curves. If we could hit his pitches, we could hit anybody's.

Nathan really was a special person. When he was born, his mother had difficulty with the delivery. Nathan's oxygen was cut-off for over two minutes. He was revived by the doctor once he was out of the birth canal and the umbilical cord was cut. It wasn't evident at the time as to how much damage, if any, had been done to his mental or physical capacity. Only time could reveal that. But it didn't take long before it was clear that Nathan would have some mental issues to face and overcome.

Unfortunately, Nathan's condition was much worse than initially thought. As he grew, his mental development managed to reach only the level of that of a four or five year old child. Nathan was about eight years older than most of the boys on our team. He was the only boy in his family, but he did have an older sister who was normal, in every way. According to his mother, Nathan had never done much socializing with other kids and pretty much had become a couch potato watching television from daylight to dark, seven days a week.

He loved to watch baseball games with his dad. When all of us boys reached that certain age and became interested in baseball, we passed ball regularly in the roadway near Nathan's home. Nathan soon got off the couch and joined us in the exercise. At first, not really knowing Nathan, we were somewhat hesitant to have him play with us. We were afraid he would not be able to catch a thrown ball and could be injured. But it was soon apparent that not only was Nathan capable of catching and throwing the baseball, he also understood the game much better than anyone could have ever imagined even though his retardation was noticeable. When all of us saw how hard and accurate he threw, we wanted him to be a part of any team we may someday put together. We were not about to make fun of him like the bridge gang did. Where Nathan was weak, we would be strong for him.

One of the things Nathan really enjoyed doing with us, besides playing baseball, was to go hiking in the nearby woods. This was especially true in autumn when the leaves on the trees were changing color and beginning to fall from the branches covering the ground like a soft blanket. The climb to the top was not easy. The slope was much too steep for building houses or even trying to farm. There was a lot of underbrush and briars that made the climb even more difficult. But once on top of the hill, on the ridge, the view over the valley was awesome. Every roof top, the Tug Fork, the highway, and all of the side roads were visible from the ridge at that time of year. In the spring and summer, that was not the case. The trees and other foliage were so thick that no one could see a damn thing. It was like a jungle up there. So just for the heck of it, we cut down several trees that were directly in front of the rock formation and topped-out a few others. It was a lot of hard work, but we were rewarded with a terrific view all year round.

A short distance around the top of the hill from where we climbed, the mountain ridge forked and went in two directions. To the left of the split was a rock formation that jutted out of the top of the hill. The rocks were divided into several large sections with hundreds of smaller pieces surrounding the larger ones. From a distance, one of the formations appeared to take the shape of a bucket. The rock was a dark grey color. The very top of the large boulder was flat with a few patches of moss and several types of vines partially covering its surface. We appropriately named the large rock "the coal bucket." We loved to climb to its summit and pretend it was our lookout for enemy soldiers that may come to invade the valley below. We had to be alert though. Sometimes venomous snakes, rattlesnakes and copperheads, liked to lie on the rocks and bath in the sunshine, but the snakes usually high-balled-it out of there whenever people came around.

The scene of looking out over the valley from up there was magnificent. All of the dirt roads running throughout the community seemed to be flat with no bumps or mud holes. The river looked to be much cleaner than what it really was and flowed smoothly under the old one lane bridge where the bridge gang appeared to be little elves sitting on the railing. The view mesmerized Nathan. He was captivated by the miniature appearance of the houses that lined both sides of the highway and dirt roads. Nathan would laugh out loud as the toy-like cars and trucks rolled through the camp and disappeared in the distance. In fact, we all enjoyed the quiet moments spent in the privacy of the forest, sitting on the coal bucket with a piece of grass or twig in mouths, lost in our thoughts and dreams that only little boys could imagine. For Nathan, those were extraordinary moments. He was an out of the ordinary person. We all were on top of the world.

THIRTEEN

The dust rose like the plume from an exploded hydrogen bomb as the pick-up trucks rolled along the dirt road carrying the Davy team from the main road to the parking area next to the field. Right behind the stream of four-wheel drives was Howard's mom delivering the lunches that would provide the energy to sustain us through the upcoming battle about to take place. While the Davy bunch did their pre-game routine, we ate our sandwiches and sweets, and relaxed in the shade of the trees that lined the playing area down the first base line while watching carefully as our opponents exposed some of their weaknesses at the plate and in the field. This was going to be one hell of a game.

Both teams had coaches. Two men coached or managed our squad. Pepper Gray was considered the head coach or manager, and Otis "Scooter" Robinson was his assistant. Scooter was the one we all called "coach." Otis had been called Scooter since he was a kid. He had always loved the game of baseball and had played in the old Negro League when he was younger. He was some 'kin to Jackie Robinson, but none of us kids knew exactly how. We think he was a third or fourth cousin. Pepper had played a lot of ball as a young man too. He led the Coalfield League in batting average and home runs for three consecutive seasons in the early 1950's. Both men enjoyed sharing their knowledge of the game with the community kids. They were just kids at heart themselves.

Finally, old man Reeves and his brother, the other old man Reeves, arrived to umpire the game. They called everyone together in a circle in the middle of the diamond just behind the pitching mound to remind us of the ground rules and of course the general playing rules, such as good sportsmanship and absolutely no cussing or fighting. We all acknowledged that we understood with a nod and under our breath, a little "screw you" verbiage from us and the Davy squad. A toss of a coin determined we would be the home team and secure the last at bat if necessary. Our team chose the first base side of the field as our dugout position. The coaches quickly gave us a final word of encouragement before we took the field to begin the ass-kicking we were about to deliver. All of us were concerned that Roy had not yet arrived. The game had to begin without him. Hopefully, the dentist hadn't pulled all of his teeth and he would get there soon, as his mom had promised. Melvin Vargis was chosen by the coaches to start at second base for Roy. That could hurt us if the opponents were able to hit Nathan's pitches. Melvin's speed and glove were great in the outfield, but Roy was a much better infielder. At any rate, we had to go with what we had for the moment.

Nathan finished his warm-up pitches, and old man Reeves (never did know what his first name was) yelled, "play ball." The first pitch was a fast ball right down the middle of the plate just above the knees. The ump cried, "Strike one." The batter never even saw the ball. This was going to be sweet. The first inning ended as planned, no runs, no hits, and no one left on base. Unfortunately, that was true for our turn at bat as well. Actually, that's the way the next four innings went. Each team had a couple of hits and two or three base runners, but neither team was able to get anyone home. It was turning into a pitching duel and defensive battle. That was totally unexpected. The first batter up in the top of the eighth swung at the first pitch from Nathan and managed a routine grounder to the second baseman. Melvin took one step toward home plate and fielded the ball cleanly. He turned toward first base and made his throw. He had plenty of time to get the runner if it wasn't for one thing. His throw was high and wide of the base. Kenneth was forced to step off the bag to avoid a more devastating result. The runner was safe. No one said it, but everyone thought it. If Roy had been there, this error would not have happened.

This shook-up Nathan a little who proceeded to walk the next two batters to load the bases with no outs. Coach Pepper called timeout and sent Coach Scooter out to talk to Nathan to settle him down a bit. When Nathan got upset, he had a tendency to cuss like a sailor, so to speak. His father was in the Navy during the war and served in the South Pacific. He had on a rare occasion shouted a word or phrase that not even the bridge gang had ever heard. But contrary to what you may think, it was his mother that did all of the cussing in their household. Boy, could she bellow it out when she was mad. Nevertheless, Nathan was about to explode, and Coach Scooter knew exactly what to say to him to prevent a confrontation with old man Reeves who had no sympathy for the mentally challenged or any other kid with a foul mouth.

"Nathan, I know you are a little disappointed with what has just happened. You probably want to cuss your guts out. But remember what the ump said about you guys cussing during the game. If he hears you say, uh, a 'dirty word' you may be kicked out of the game, and that would be worse than walking a couple of batters to load the bases. Right?"

"Yeah, I guess," Nathan replied.

"Okay then. You don't cuss. Let me do the cussing this time. You just concentrate on getting the next three pussies out. And remember, don't be afraid to let them hit the ball. You have a lot of good fielders behind you that can get these guys out too. Now let's play ball," Coach shouted.

That's all it took for Nathan. Just a word or two of encouragement and he was ready to "get after it." And that's exactly what he did. The next batter was called out on strikes with only three pitches. Then the following batter popped-up to the catcher on the first pitch. And the final out came on a grounder to me at third that I fielded on one hop and then stepped on the base for the force. Now, all we had to do was to somehow score a run and then hold them for three more outs. The deed would be accomplished. Not quite an ass-kicking but a win nonetheless.

Raymond was the leadoff batter for us in the bottom half of the eighth inning. So far for the day, he had struck out twice and grounded out to shortstop. The first pitch was high and inside for ball one. Raymond swung at the next two pitches fouling both of them off. He stepped out of the batter's box for a moment to settle his nerves. He then stepped back in ready for the next pitch. The pitcher went into his motion and delivered what looked like a fast ball headed for the inside part of the plate. Raymond started to swing, but held up thinking, "I'm sure this pitch is going to miss inside for ball two." However, the pitch was actually a slider that broke over the plate at the last second. It would have surely been called strike three if Raymond's bat had not been extended as he fell backwards, away from the plate. The ball came off of the bat much like a bunted ball would do and rolled down the third base line. Raymond quickly recovered and ran as hard as he could to first base. The pitcher sprung from the mound, and the third baseman charged from third converging on the slow rolling sphere. Both were determined to pick it up and throw the ball in time to get the out at first. However, as they each reached for the ball, they collided, knocking each other to the ground without a chance of fielding the ball and completing a play at first base. This was the break we had been looking for. All we had to do was take full advantage of it. However, the coaches had a big decision to make. The next batter due up was Nathan. If a pinch hitter was used, Nathan would have to come out of the game. He was still pitching strong, and removing him now could be a big mistake. No one on our team could come close to throwing like Nathan.

After a brief discussion, Coach Pepper spoke to Nathan, and then sent him to the plate. Raymond was not a threat to steal second, and with Nathan at the plate, the hit and run was not a good option. So the next best thing to try, don't swing at anything. Nathan just stood there and looked at each pitch. It almost worked. He was called out on strikes but only after taking the count to 3-2 (three balls and two strikes). At least a possible double play was avoided.

Howard, our leadoff batter, was up next. He swung at the first pitch and hit it on the button, a hard liner to the shortstop for the second out. Now we needed a string of hits, an extra base hit, or a long ball over the fence, anything to get Raymond around the bases and in to score. Before the game started, no one would have guessed that either team would have gone this deep into the game without scoring a bunch of runs. Yet, here we were deadlocked at 0-0, and it appeared that we would head into the ninth inning scoreless.

Bill Vargis stepped into the batter's box. He and the pitcher had a couple of words for one another when old man Reeves intervened with a few words of his own. Bill looked determined. The first pitch was a ball. The second caught the outside of the plate for a strike. Bill stepped out to collect himself. Then back into the box. The pitch was on its way. Bill swung with a grunt, and the ball was lined hard over the third baseman's head into left field for a hit. The ball was actually hit too hard and was quickly retrieved by the left fielder. He made a quick and accurate throw to third to hold Raymond at second.

Now it was my time to try to keep the inning going. I had hit the ball all three times in my previous at bats, but each one had been caught for outs. Obviously, I was a little bummed over my performance so far. Just like most of our batters, I too took the first pitch. It was a strike. Right down the middle of the plate. There was no way I was going to see another pitch like that. Wow. As the pitcher went into his delivery of the next pitch from the mound, I squared around in a bunting position hoping to draw the third baseman in a step or two. If he did charge hard, it would take a perfect and swift throw to get me at first. There was a good chance he would not make a throw knowing that Raymond would be on the move from second and could score if his throw was errant.

Just like a well written script, the third baseman broke for the plate in anticipation of a bunt. But, as the ball reached the plate, I swung the bat and punched the ball in the air toward third and over the charging fielder's head, dropping the ball into no man's land. The left fielder raced to the ball and hurriedly tossed it back to the infield. Raymond was speeding from second and slid into third without a tag. Vargis was now on second. I was safe at first. The bases were loaded with our clean-up hitter coming to the plate. Buddy was the right person to have at bat in this situation: bases loaded, two out, and the game on the line. Buddy had doubled earlier in the game with two out, and we couldn't get him home.

The Davy coaches called for a timeout and headed to the pitching mound for a conference with the pitcher and infielders. After a lengthy discussion the coaches decided to stay with their starting pitcher just as our team had done with Nathan in the top half of the inning. The coaches returned to the third base side of the field. Old man Reeves signaled to play ball. The pitcher went into his wind-up and set the ball in flight toward the plate. Buddy was in his batter's stance with his back foot dug-in, the bat held high over his back shoulder. As the ball approached, the bat left Buddy's shoulder in a swift downward then upward motion, connecting with the ball and sending it high into the air toward the left field fence some three hundred and forty feet away from home plate. Everyone stood in awe wondering if it had enough distance to clear the fence. It seemed like forever before the ball fell from the sky about ten to twenty feet beyond the fence. Buddy had done it, a grand slam home run. Raymond, Bill, and I jumped around the bases and waited with the rest of the team who had gathered at the plate cheering Buddy as he touched home plate to give us a four run lead. It was just like a fairy tale come true.

After a Davy pitching change, Hubert grounded out second to first for the third out of the inning. Now, all we had to do was hold them to fewer than four runs, get three outs, and the victory would be ours. Needless to say, the Davy squad was a little shell shocked and went out with three up and three down in the top of the ninth. Mission accomplished. Coach Pepper and Coach Scooter were just as excited over the win as all of the boys. They promised to buy all of us a hot dog, French fries, and a coke at Stella's Store when we got back to the community. This moment felt like Christmas.

But where was Roy? He had missed playing in the best baseball game of the summer. "Man, will he be pissed," we all thought.

FOURTEEN

Standing in front of Stella's Store, we were all talking at once, only half listening to what the other was saying, still excited about the big victory over the more experienced Davy baseball team. Stella and her husband had our orders for hot (chili) dogs and were working feverishly to get them made, then collect the money from the coaches, and get all of us the hell out of there. Stella and Tiny (that was her husband's name, Tiny, who weighed well over three hundred pounds) operated a small convenience store where the community could pickup milk, bread, cigarettes, and other common items used around the house. It was convenient because the adults could have us kids run to the store for them to get those frequently needed things. Unfortunately, Stella didn't make French fries. Instead, we had to settle for potato chips.

Finishing off the last of the dogs and chips, Raymond asked me to go with him to Roy's house and find out why the little turd was a no show for the game. I declined and told Raymond to go it alone, and then to let me know what he found out. I bet there was a good explanation, but I could not begin to guess what it was. For now though, I had to high-ball-it to my house and take a much needed shit. Those dogs went right through me. Some of the other guys made a quick departure as well for the same reason. Stella must have put some extra ingredients in her special chili.

I had just come out of the bathroom leaving behind some pretty serious methane gas when someone knocked on the front door. Before mom could get up from her living room chair and lay the newspaper aside, the knock echoed through the house again.

"Alright, I'm coming. Hold your horses," mom shouted. She reached for the doorknob, but before she tightened her grip, the door flung open. Raymond came bursting in, breathing heavy, and his voice screeching something that no one could understand.

"Calm down, Raymond. Catch your breath and talk slowly," mom suggested.

"It's Roy, its Roy, he's gone," Raymond managed to bark.

"What do you mean, he's gone?" mom and I asked in unison.

"No one knows where he is," Raymond replied.

"Okay, let's take this one step at a time, Raymond. What are you trying to tell us? Take it slow, and start from the beginning so we can follow what you are saying," mom instructed.

Raymond explained, "I left Stella's and headed to Roy's to see why he hadn't made it to the game. When I got there, his mom and dad were in the front yard. I went up to them and asked where Roy was. Roy's dad said he thought he was with us guys. I told them that after our game we had gone for hot dogs at Stella's. No one had seen Roy. He was not at the game. His mom immediately went into a hissy fit and started crying and hollering that something bad had happened to Roy. That damn, I mean, darn near scared me to death."

"Is that all that was said?" asked mom.

"No, Mr. Smith said when they got home from the trip to the dentist that Roy grabbed his ball glove and ran out of the house. He said he was going straight to the ball field. He did not want to be late for the game," Raymond stated, wide-eyed. "Mr. Smith then told me to get the team together and go looking for Roy. If we found him or anything like his glove or shirt or something, then hurry back and let our parents or the coaches know immediately. Mrs. Smith ran into the house and called the police. She was talking with them when I left to come here. Roy's dad started following the path that Roy would have taken to get to the field as fast as he could. He was headed toward the trestle."

"You boys go to the school grounds and wait for the coaches and the other boys to get there. I will start calling their parents and get a calling chain started to help speed up the process and reach as many people in the neighborhood as swiftly as possible. The more people looking for Roy make the possibility of finding him quickly much better," mom said as she reached for the telephone. Raymond and I headed for the schoolyard.

When we reached the schoolyard, some of the guys that lived closer to the school than me had already arrived. Mom had called their homes and told their parents a brief summary of what was going on. It was only a few minutes before the rest of the team including the coaches were there. Some of the fathers and mothers of the guys also came to help search for Roy. Coach Gray took charge and began to snap orders like some half-crazed Marine Sergeant. But that was good. He was like that – organized. No one was offended. We all just listened and did what he said.

We split up into four search teams or squads as Coach Pep called them. We often referred to Coach Pepper as just Coach Pep. Five of us were in Coach Scooter's group. There was Buddy, Raymond, Alex, Louie, and me. Alex was Roy's next door neighbor and played ball with us from time to time. He had not played in our game with

Davy because of some function going on at his church. His mom would not allow him to miss it. Alex and Louie were the only two black kids on the team, and Louie was a first cousin of Flick's. It was only natural that Louie would be in the same search party as me.

"Well, one thing we are pretty sure of, there were no trains through here today that we are aware of. At least none passed by the ball field while we were there," Coach Gray began. "There is only about an hour and a half of day light remaining. So, let's cover as much territory as possible before it gets dark. If we need to, the search can continue with flashlights; but, you boys will have to have permission from your parents to be out here after dark unless at least one of them accompanies you," Coach Gray made clear.

"Let's start at the trestle with two teams climbing down the embankment on each side of the tracks and two teams crossing the trestle and going down the embankments on the opposite side of the gorge. Look thoroughly on the hillside as you make your way to the bottom just in case Roy has fallen from the tracks and could be injured and unable to get our attention. If you spot anything at all, let the rest of the groups know so we can all concentrate looking in the same area and maybe locate Roy quickly," Coach Gray said delicately.

Buddy and I took the lead as we started over the rim of the steep terrain that would take us to the river's edge far below the towering bridge of wood and iron. Even though we were tough, agile kids, each of us had to be extremely careful with our descent. A slight slip could send us tumbling head over heels in a downward plunge that could easily break every bone in our body. The adults were constantly bellowing, "Be cautious and watch your step. We don't want anyone to get hurt and have to be carried back up this slippery slope on a stretcher." I thought,

"How the hell are we going to get Roy out of here if he's here and seriously injured? Tie a rope to his legs and all of us pull him up? Give me a break."

Mr. Smith made his way to the trestle ahead of us. He was on the river bank below when we arrived. He, too, waved to us and echoed the command to be careful coming down the slope. He seemed to be holding up well considering his son had just gone missing. I wondered how my real mother might be feeling right now. Does she ever go looking for me? Does she have anyone to help her search? Does she miss me? Has she given up?

We combed the hillside thoroughly from top to bottom inspecting any disturbance that looked remotely suspicious. No sign of Roy or any other living or dead creature. I was surprised we had not yet run across at least one snake or rat. We walked up and down both sides of the river not seeing any evidence that anyone had been along the river for quite some time. We did see pieces of old fishing line and a few discarded soda cans. Each can was badly rusted indicating they had been there for awhile. If Roy had fallen into the river from above, he would have to be stuck in the mud on the bottom of the river. Not a pleasant thought.

It was nearing dusk when the Rescue Squad and State Police arrived on the scene. The trooper in charge confirmed there was no train traffic in our area that day. He thanked all of us for searching and ordered all of the young adults, as he put it, to return to their homes. Any adults that wished to continue looking would be assigned to a member of the ten-man rescue squad who would direct the search efforts into the night. They wanted to extend the hunt along the tracks from the trestle all the way to the ball diamond. All of us guys were disappointed we could not remain. However, we followed the trooper's instructions and started back home.

A short distance from the train trestle near the first bend in the tracks, we stopped. Some of us guys sat on the tracks while others stood. We were all shocked and saddened by Roy's disappearance. What could have happened to Roy? Our theories were as numerous and scattered as the many pointed stars that were beginning to appear in the heavens above us. However, the one thought that all of us had, but no one wanted to express openly, was unequivocally uttered by Louie, "Somebody got him."

FIFTEEN

We sat and talked as the daylight faded. We were frustrated that nothing had turned up on Roy's whereabouts. It was time for all of us to start for home to keep our parents from sending out search parties for us. I was sure they would want some news or update on what was going on with the search. We all agreed to get together first thing in the morning by meeting at this very spot at eight o'clock and continue to canvass the area, if nothing was resolved overnight.

Buddy, Raymond, and I were the last of the group to leave. We only walked a few steps when Raymond asked, "Did you guys hear that?"

"Hear what?" I asked.

"There, I heard it," Buddy remarked. "It sounds like someone is walking on the gravel between the tracks. They're headed this way."

"Maybe its Roy," exclaimed Raymond.

"Well one thing is for sure, it's not a group of people. It appears to be only one person or thing," I responded.

"There you go with that spooky crap again," Buddy hissed.

"Up yours, jerk-weed," I countered.

"All right, all right, just shut up. Whatever or whoever it is, is about here. Quick, let's hide in the brush and wait to see who it is," Buddy retorted.

The three of us quickly jumped into the brush and squatted down to avoid being seen. The moonlight was now providing enough illumination for good visibility for a rather long distance of maybe twenty-five or thirty yards. It was only a few seconds after our dive into the weeds when a figure appeared, coming around the bend in the center of the tracks. It was the outline of a man. He was wearing bibbed overalls and a light weight jacket that looked to be very worn and torn in several places. On his head was a baseball cap, so dirty the team logo was not distinguishable. His boots were only partially laced and were in need of a cobbler's touch. He was carrying an old flour sack over his shoulder that was about half full of something. It didn't appear to be too heavy.

As he came near, we all recognized him. It was the man we all knew as "Sister Brooks." I think his real name was Tom Brooks, but I had only heard him referred to as "Sister Brooks" or just "the Sister" for short. He wasn't seen much out in the community, but from time to time he could be observed walking along the roadway or along the railroad tracks. Usually he carried a sack or a box filled with mushrooms or ramps he had dug up from along the hillside somewhere nearby. He kept to himself and had no family or friends that we knew of. He didn't want any friends or handouts, as he had so directly stated to the church minister many times when the church outreach program offered him clothing and food. He seemed to get-by okay on his own, and no one had any issues with him, except the fact he was always in need of a shave, a bath, and not surprisingly, deodorant.

Of course, there were those stories, whether true or not, that are always attached to a person like "the Sister." One such story that made a lasting impression with all of the kids was that Sister Brooks loved to eat dogs. Not a Stella hot dog, but dogs. Anytime someone's dog or other pet turned up missing, we would say that "the Sister" must have needed to restock his pantry. As far as we knew, there was no evidence he ever did really kill or eat anyone's pet. But we kept our dogs and cats as far away from his place as possible. He was just weird.

After Brooks passed-by and turned away from the tracks in the direction of where he lived, we came out of our hideout, brushed off our clothing, and breathed a sigh of relief. When we were certain the coast was clear, we set out for home with a brisk walk that soon exploded into an all out sprint.

The next morning I was up at the crack of dawn and hurriedly got dressed. I reached for a slice of bread, popped it into the toaster, and somewhat impatiently, waited for the metamorphosis to take place. I added the condiments of butter and strawberry jelly, and then devoured the hearty breakfast of champions with a tall, cold glass of milk. It would hold me for most of the day. The excitement of rejoining the search for Roy and the anticipation of finding some clue of where he might be were enough to the hold the appetite at bay.

I met up with Buddy and Raymond near the school grounds. Buddy said his dad had left the house early that morning to meet with other adults eager to get started. Many of the adults had been out all night and were coming in for some food and a short rest before resuming their search efforts. Since it was Sunday, some of the folks thought it would be appropriate to stop the search for a brief period and spend the time in the church on our knees praying. But the pastor of the church suggested the time should be spent looking for Roy while it was still daylight. He said people could and should pray continually while they searched. Everyone that attended church agreed. Both the morning and the evening services were cancelled. However, for anyone who was physically unable to join the search, the church was left open for use at their convenience.

The three of us started out in the direction of the trestle. Along the way we were joined by Howard. The group that Howard was a part of the night before had combed the area under the trestle across the river from where the rest of us had been. He said there wasn't a sign of any living thing on that side of the river. The only thing he noticed was the terrible smell of human feces floating in the river.

"Pity the poor soul that falls into that sewer," he said. "If he doesn't drown, the stench will suffocate him. Either way, it's a shitty way to go."

We decided to broaden our search and cover the vicinity beyond the trestle along the tracks to the ball field. A quick canvas of the area was completed on Saturday evening with no luck. We knew if Roy had to stop to take a leak, but we all knew that he didn't, he would have done so in the weeds off from the tracks along this path.

The remainder of the day was spent covering every inch of ground from Roy's home to the ball diamond. The Sheriff's Deputies had now joined the hunt after waiting a twenty-four hour period required by department policy on missing persons. The State Police and the Rescue Squad were all out in full force. They helped to cover the regions along the tracks and the highway, an alternate, but a much longer way to the field. There's no way Roy would have chosen to follow the highway with his teammates anticipating his prompt arrival.

The police spent much of the day interviewing people in the community who might have seen or heard something unusual on Saturday. They even went to Sister Brooks' house to talk with him. Louie, who didn't live too far from the Sister's shack, said the police actually went into the Sister's place and looked around for a long time.

As far as he knew, the search didn't turn up anything. But we all thought it was sure strange for the police to choose his place to go into and look around. They didn't do that at any other house.

The day came to an end with the same result as on the day before. The next day was Monday. The majority of us kids headed off to school. Over the next few weeks, we all kind of settled back into our normal routines. The search for Roy came to a halt with no sign or clue of where he was. His family slowly retreated into their own little world with very little contact with the neighbors. It was just before Christmas when they suddenly moved out of their home and went back to Ohio. Mrs. Smith looked like a ghost. She had lost all kinds of weight. Mr. Smith was absent from work a lot after Roy went missing. The mining company out of sympathy for the family offered him a severance package along with a Christmas bonus and then, quietly let him go. It was all so sad. When I was taken from my real mother, she must have had the same feeling of loss as Mr. and Mrs. Smith. I wanted to say something to them, to let them know that I knew how they felt. But I couldn't find the courage or the words. Besides, I'm not sure they would have believed me. I simply waved good-bye.

SIXTEEN

After Roy's disappearance and the subsequent failure to locate him or determine how or why he had vanished, I spent many evenings over a plate of cookies and a glass of milk imparting to myself the irony of my adoption journey so far. I was ordered by the court to be removed from a mother that probably could not provide a safe and normal, purely subjective mind you, environment to a family that could. Let's see. So far two of my best friends have been either murdered or kidnapped, there's a weirdo loose in the community, the bridge gang still does their thing, some of my make-believe relatives treat me like shit when mom and dad are not around, and no one seems to know anything about my past or just won't say. Need I say more? What a paradox.

But I have to say there were times, many times, I did feel like a real member of this adoptive family. Like the time I received my first bicycle. Actually, it was the only bike I ever had. It's still in the basement of our home right now. It was a surprise gift for Christmas when I was eight years old, just a little over a week before my ninth birthday. The size of the bike was referred to as a twenty-four inch bike. The bike's frame was smaller than the twenty-six inch bikes many of the community kids were riding, but it seemed to fit my short legs just fine. The bicycle was bright red. It was made by Roll-Fast, a company none of us kids had ever heard of. It came equipped with a headlight and horn. Well, dad added the light and horn as extras. All I had to do was to learn how to ride the darn thing.

Naturally, that particular winter was a harsh one with plenty of snow and cold, freezing temperatures that kept the ground blanketed well into the early spring. It didn't look like I was ever going to have an opportunity to even attempt to ride my new set of wheels. But like it is with most things, the cold weather passed. The winter finally lost its grip as the snow began to melt with the rising temperatures. March, like the Saints, went marching on with its winds blowing past April fool's day and finally drying up most of the mud, remnants of frozen moisture that kept the new shiny tandem garaged in a warm, dry place for three months.

Then, one afternoon shortly after returning home from a day at school, dad said, "Okay, let's get on with it. Let the bike out of its confinement, and let's see how you do with your first riding lesson."

It almost sounded like he was referring to riding a horse instead of a bike. But I sure as hell knew what he meant. I didn't waste any time rushing to the basement, kicking the kick-stand to a raised position, and escorting the thoroughbred to the starting gate (although in my mind it was more like driving a high performance coupé to the starting line of the Grand Prix). Nevertheless, it was a dirt training track that lay before us. Dad was waiting there with a big smile on his face. I, too, was smiling from ear to ear.

As I rolled up to where dad was standing, he reached out and took control of the bike. He straddled the rear tire and fender to keep the bike upright while pointing and instructing me on how to mount the stallion. He explained how to place the hands on the handle bar grips and to swing a leg over the seat and frame, placing the foot of that leg on the bicycle's pedal located on the opposite side of the bike from where the body was positioned. Next, I could start moving forward by pushing off with my foot that was still on the ground and bearing the bulk of my weight. Once moving, my body could be centered over the frame of the bike with both feet placed on pedals and ready to accelerate down the track. Of course, until I was able to maintain my balance on the two-wheeled vehicle, he provided the help for me to remain afloat by following along behind and holding the seat to keep the bike upright as I rode and steered. It seemed easy enough. And it was easy as long as he held on to the seat.

After several afternoons of practice, I began to get the hang of it. Frequently, Dad released his grip on the seat and allowed me to glide solo for a short distance. This process worked as long as I was unaware I was solo. When I did notice dad not keeping up, I would wobble. He had to hurry to my rescue before I crashed. He always said I could ride without any assistance. I just needed the confidence I could do it. It was a mindset thing at this point he argued.

But mom wanted to make sure I had a lot more practice before turning me loose all alone on "that thing" as she called it. So, for awhile, she took over as the trainer in charge and stepped into dad's roll of holding up the bike, as I continued to become more proficient in remaining balanced. After only a couple of days with mom helping out, and providing much encouragement, the time finally arrived. What started out as a typical ride-along, with mom trotting behind, her hand on the seat, was soon an unaccompanied, on your own, by yourself experience that lifted my confidence to new heights. I was cruising all alone. I looked back. I saw mom standing with one hand on her stomach and the other covering her mouth. She was more frightened than I was. I suddenly became a little apprehensive. Could I turn this thing around all by myself without laying it down on its side? I was about to find out.

I made the approach to the right side of the road. I then turned the front wheel to the left, leaning slightly to the inside, trying to maintain enough speed to keep the bike moving. I managed to maneuver through the one-hundred-eighty degree turn without falling and was now heading back in the direction of where mom was left standing a minute or so before. I did it. Mom no longer had her hands on her stomach or mouth. She was now clapping and cheering me on as I passed by her, feeling the wind in my face and an excitement I had never before experienced.

Then everything started to change. I realized that just ahead was another turning opportunity. This turn was definitely going to be different. The road was not as wide, so the turn would require a shorter radius and was on a slightly down hill slope. The turning area was smack dab in front of my Uncle Dustan's house; and, wouldn't you know it, he was standing on his front porch watching my progress with much interest. But what the heck, I had just made one turn on my own. "This one should be just as easy to negotiate," I told myself.

Then the unthinkable happened. As I guided the bike to the right to make another left-hand turn, the pedal on the right side made contact with my uncle's fence. The impact caused the bike to momentarily hesitate and then lurch forward. I was losing control of the bike. I quickly and instinctively turned the front tire to the right to regain stability. The bicycle straightened, but only for a moment. There just wasn't enough space between the bike and my uncle's chain-linked fence to accommodate my tactical adjustment. The entire right side of the bike, including my right leg, collided with the fence, ricocheted, and went crashing to the ground.

"Are you hurt? Are you okay?" mom shouted repetitively as she came rushing to my aid.

"I'm okay!" I quickly exclaimed trying to avoid

further embarrassment of being cuddled in front of my uncle. The mishap was embarrassing enough by itself.

My uncle also reacted quickly by leaping from his porch, hurrying over to his fence, and making a spontaneous assessment of the damages. To his surprise and obvious disappointment, the fence appeared to be unscathed. But he did seem to enjoy pointing out that both the headlamp and horn on my bike were not so fortunate. The light was broken. The horn was bent near its center to almost a ninety degree angle. When the horn's rubber ball-like end was squeezed, the horn did not make a honking sound or anything near the sound a horn is expected to make. Only the swooshing sound of air being forced through the tubing was audible. My uncle laughed as I tested the horn's performance to no avail.

Mom was "Johnny on the spot" though with assuring my uncle that, "He doesn't need the light or the horn anyway. Those are for sissies and he ain't a sissy. By the way, is Seth's light and horn still working on his bike?"

My uncle appeared to be dumbfounded by mom's comeback. He turned abruptly and walked hurriedly to his front door, entered his house, and slammed the door shut behind him.

It was true. I didn't mind not having a light or horn on the bike. I was happy just having a bicycle. In addition to the two ornament casualties, the front fender also sustained a few scratches. Mom said dad could touch up those marks with a little paint. The fender would look like new. I assured her it was not necessary to repair any of the scrapes. It was okay the way it was. The wounded fender added character. With just a few more noticeable dings and scratches, it would look more like the used bike Flick was learning to ride. She was okay with that.

SEVENTEEN

I did not become a teenager until midway through my eighth grade school year. Kids from Big Sandy attended junior high and high school in Welch. The school was referred to as a high school, but it was really a combination junior high and high school made-up of grades seven through twelve. The seventh grade was a year of major transition. No longer did we sit in one classroom all day and listen to only one teacher. Now we had to follow a class schedule, defined by the subject matter being taught in the class, and change classrooms and teachers every hour. For those commuting by school bus, a school day was a long, often stressful day approaching twelve hours. To accommodate the bus arrivals from a number of feeder grade schools from contiguous locations to the county seat, the start of morning classes was determined by a staggered schedule beginning at 7:30, 8:30, or 9:30 A.M. At mid-day, there was a half-hour lunch break on a spread out timetable as well. The school day concluded between 2:00 and 4:00 P.M., unless there was football or basketball practice. Throw in the morning time spent getting ready for school and the travel time to and from school and there's the damn twelve hours.

The arrival of autumn brought a sense of sadness. School was in session, which meant more long days for those who rode a school bus, not leaving much time after school to socialize with your friends. However, there was some excitement that came with the beginning of the new school year. There was the renewal of friendships with kids that lived in other communities and had not been in touch since school was out for the summer. And, there were also fresh opportunities to meet new students. Some moved in from other counties, states, and a few from time to time from other countries. It was always exciting to make new friends and share learning experiences. But what was really special was seeing the old friends from the previous year and laughing about all the dumb shit we went through during the summer, like family picnics and reunions. It's funny looking back on it. We always talked about the things that bored us more than the good things we experienced: like special vacations, daily freedoms of swimming in the river, running through the woods, seeing women sunbathing naked in their backyards behind so called privacy fences.

One of the dreaded eighth grade classes was American History. The reason for the trepidation was not so much the subject but the teacher, Ms. Fox. Believe me, she was no fox. She was an old maid that found great pleasure in assigning loads of homework and then chewing the hell out of you when you came to class with the work incomplete. The bitch was meaner than any D.I. (drill instructor) ever thought of being. There were only two history classes available to eighth grade students. The good news was there was a fifty-fifty chance you might get the easier teacher, the meek and mild, Miss Sampson. The bad news was I wasn't so lucky. My assignment was to the Fox torture-chamber.

The class was made up of about thirty-two students. The girls outnumbered the boys by two, seventeen to fifteen. I thought most of the kids in the class were my friends, but there were a few I wasn't really sure of. Jackie Preston was one of those. I don't know how it was that

Jackie and I wanted to kick each other's asses so much, but that's the way it was since we met in the seventh grade. He was from one of those well-to-do Welch families that looked down on people from what they considered poorer communities. Big Sandy was one of those poor locations. From the very beginning of our encounter with each other, if there was a line drawn for any reason, you could bet Jackie and I would be standing on opposite sides of it.

And also, there were kids who were neither my friends nor my rivals. They weren't anything to me, and I wasn't anything to them. They could care less about me and me about them. When class was in session, they were just there, faces in a classroom, occupying seats. We very seldom saw each other when school was not in session. They didn't ride my bus, and I had no idea where they lived. They simply disappeared when school was out.

There was one newcomer in the history class. The boy's name was Aaron. His family moved to Welch from somewhere in Virginia. His dad worked for the telephone company and was transferred to the McDowell County location over the summer. Aaron was a tall, thin kid who just happened to be starting puberty. He had a high-pitched voice that cracked when he least expected. That always enticed a few laughs from the class. He was quick-tempered and soon drew the wrath of Ms. Fox when he shouted during class one day for everyone to shut the hell up. Needless to say, Aaron made several trips to the Principal's office for, what was called, counseling for his use of bad language.

We soon became good friends. At first, Aaron missed his former classmates from Virginia. He loved to debate Civil War issues in history class and was proud to be from one of the Confederate states. When he learned I was born in Virginia, and later moved to West Virginia, and then adopted, he took interest in my situation, forming a bond based on southern brotherhood, so to speak. I introduced Aaron to the rest of the gang at school.

We weren't a real gang. We were just a bunch of kids who were drawn together for various reasons and shared a lot of things in common. Most of the kids at school were part of clicks, small groups of classmates that chose to hang-out together at lunch and if lucky, to have a few classes or study hall together. There were a few groups though that thought they were bona fide gangs and called all of the shots around school. They quickly learned who they could rule and push around and those that would resist and fight back. Believe it or not, there were only a few wimps at our school, and most of those lived in the town of Welch. The kids from outside of town were mostly from working class homes. They didn't take shit from anybody.

Our troupe was comprised of Eddie, Mark, Craig, me, and now, Aaron. The five of us had two things in common – poverty and the ignorance that we were so poor. If our small ensemble had a leader, it was probably Eddie. He was by far the strongest of the five, open and honest, and the one person, who if forced to fight, would kick your ass every day of the week and twice on Sundays – then spend half of a day explaining how sorry he was for what he did to you. He was also the only one of us that had a steady girl friend in eighth grade.

Mark was the cool member, always with a cigarette in his mouth (not in class of course, although he would have if he could have gotten away with it). He had an answer for everything, which usually ended with, "eat shit and bark at the moon."

Craig was the innocent one of our group. He didn't know anything about anything. That in no way meant he didn't want to learn. He was continually asking the questions: how, what, when, where, and why. He never got the answers to his questions from us. His ignorance, or innocence, humored us all.

Then there was Hank, not part of our core but the older brother of Jackie Preston. Hank was held back a couple of times in grade school. He wasn't the sharpest nail in the keg and by his family's standards, an embarrassment. He was not particularly fond of being in the same grade as his brother. The school's administration did manage to place them in separate classes to avoid discord as much as possible. However, conflicts seemed to find Hank quite easily. He was always, I mean always, looking for a fight. Because he was older than the rest of us, he was a bit crazy about showing his muscle and issuing threats to stay out of his way or else. He also had a crush on Eddie's girlfriend, Robin. No one actually talked about it, but we all knew it was just a matter of time before Eddie and Hank would come to grips with the true meaning of chivalry.

EIGHTEEN

Leaving grade school and entering junior high school in the fall of 1960 at the age of eleven was a daunting experience. Most kids entering junior high were already twelve or thirteen years old. I had to wait until January before celebrating my twelfth birthday. Many of the other boys in seventh grade were an inch or two taller and ten to twenty pounds heavier than me. I guess starting school at age five had its disadvantages too. However, the seventh grade opened a whole new chapter in my life. I was finally able to be close to my real-blood brother. Since the junior high and high schools shared the same campus, I could meet with my brother during lunch and on occasion after school.

I didn't waste any time in looking for my brother. I spent the first three days during the lunch hour running all over the property searching for him. Finally, on the fourth day, I saw him, just outside the building where the principal's office was located, sitting on a rock wall near the flag pole, having lunch with a girl. As I approached, he spotted me and beckoned me to join them. I ran to where they were as fast as my short legs would carry me.

Up until now, my brother and I had not had an opportunity to spend any quality time together. Right after I learned of my adoption and that I actually had a brother, his adoptive parents brought him to my house for a visit. Unfortunately, the evening they decided to drop-by, I had gone on a weekend camping trip with some neighbors and missed meeting him. Likewise, my mom and dad took me to see him a few weeks after his failed visit only to discover he was out of town for a few days with an uncle and aunt. It didn't seem like our meeting one another was destined to be.

However, during the summer between my fifth and sixth grades, the time did come, in the disguise of a chance meeting, when our families ran into each other (not literally) while shopping for groceries at the Kroger Store in Welch. While the grown-ups shopped, my brother and I went outside and got to know each other (sort of). At first, it was somewhat awkward trying to make conversation. After all, he was five (almost six) years older than me. Nevertheless, with his coaxing, we were able to carve out a few meaningful sentences that led to some laughs and warm sibling moments. Our meeting was cut short by the return of our parents with the groceries and the urgency of getting all the frozen foods delivered home and placed in the freezer. We left that first encounter with his promise to share further what he could remember about our family before the death of our father and the taking away of all of the children from our birth mother. I knew he had a lot he wanted to say. I could sense he was as glad as I was to have someone to say it to that would listen.

"Hey, little brother, how have you been? It's good to see you," he said as I approached the two of them.

"How you liking school so far?"

"Oh, school's okay, I guess. I miss recess though," I replied.

"Don't you have a study hall period?" he asked.

"Yeah, I do. It's the last period of the day," I answered.

"Well, that's your recess…especially if it's your last class of the day. Just skip the period and get out early," he said jokingly.

"Are you kidding? You eleventh grade scholars may be able to get away with skipping class but not us lowly junior high dummies. Anyway, I don't want to get into trouble with the principal. I hear he's one mean character," I responded with a grin.

"Naw, he's not so tough. But, if you do have to face him, just tell him that you get your mischievousness honestly…from your brother. That will blow his mind."

We both laughed.

"Oh, I almost forgot. This is my friend, Dianna. Dianna, this is my younger brother," he seemed to say proudly as he introduced us.

"It's great to finally meet you. I've heard so much about you," she said ostensibly. How could that be, I thought. My brother hardly knows me, so how could there be that much to tell.

"All good I hope," I responded with the only thing I could think to say.

"Of course it's all good. You don't think your brother would say anything but nice things, do you?"

"How could he? He don't know shit, I mean, jack about me," I said letting the "s" word slip at an inappropriate time.

"See, I told you he was an all good kid," my brother quickly inserted as they both laughed at my blunder.

"Are you my brother's girlfriend?"

"Well, we are very good friends, but we don't date on any regular basis. So, I guess you could say we are not really boy friend, girl friend like you are probably asking," she explained.

"It was good to meet you. I have to get going and eat some lunch before the bell rings," I said trying to end this nonsense conversation.

"Okay, little brother, good to see you. I'll be in

touch. You study hard so you get some good grades...unlike your brother," he said as I departed.

Thank goodness she was not his steady date or anything. Hopefully, he and I would be able to link-up for some visits maybe on the weekends. And that's exactly what we did. Over the next year and a half, before my brother graduated in the spring of 1962, we spent many weekends together. Not as many as I would have liked, but several laudable ones.

One of the more memorable occasions was one when he came for an all day visit early on a Saturday morning. We spent much of the morning shooting basketball and passing baseball in the back yard. We did some talking about the past, but most of the conversation was on current stuff like: what sport does each of us like best; what's our favorite baseball team; who's going to go to the World Series; what kind of friends do we have; do we like girls; etc. There was some attempt to bring up the past about our family, but we had to keep our voices low for my fear of upsetting my mom if she happened to overhear us.

"What does she expect us to talk about?" my brother pondered out loud. "What the weather is supposed to be?"

After a lunch of peanut butter and jelly sandwiches (I was pleased that my brother liked the same kind of sandwich as me), we went out for a long walk. Actually, the long walk turned into a hike up the side of the hill to the ridge and then around the mountain top in the direction of the "coal bucket." Once we made it to the rock formation, we looked around for any snakes that might be warming in the sun and then climbed up the sides of the huge bolder to reach the uppermost surface. This was the first glimpse my brother had had of the panoramic view of my community. He was totally amazed with what he saw. I pointed out such strategic locations as the bridge, the grade school, some of my friend's houses, and my house. He thought it was a great get away place where us kids could come and play. He said it was serene.

"What does serene mean?" I remember asking.

"It means tranquil," he said.

"What does tranquil mean?" I had to inquire.

"It means calm and peaceful or quiet and still," he again explained with a chuckle.

We both sat down on the edge of the rock and looked out over the valley.

My brother began to talk. "You know, kid, I sometimes wish we were still a family. But times were awful tough for us back then. I remember our father was sick a lot and our mom had to keep us kids all quiet so he could get his rest. I don't know what was wrong with him, but I know he was several years older than our mother. He was married once before he met our mom. His first wife died, so he and our mom got married and started a family. He had some children by the first marriage. All of them were grown when we were born. I don't think his first family was happy with his decision to remarry. They never came around to visit as I remember; and, they never offered any help when things got rough for all of us after dad died."

"But why did the court and judge take us away from our mother and separate us from each other?" I asked angrily and confused.

"Our mother did not have a job. She had no way to support a family. She did not finish high school. She had no skills outside that of being a wife and caring mother. Even if she did have a job like cleaning houses or such, there was no one to watch us kids while she had to be away; and, the truth is, your brother needed watching twenty-four hours a day," he continued.

"There was one time not long before our father

passed away when I was playing all alone on the road near our little house. It was a dirt road. There was only four or five houses near-by. I don't know why I did it, but I picked up a rock and threw it right through a large picture window with a man sitting just inside near the window reading a newspaper. I'm not sure if I was trying to hit the man or just wanted to break the window. All I do know is the man was extremely mad and threatened to kill me. I ran home as fast as I could. Dad came out and talked with the man for a long period of time. When they were finished, dad came back into the house and went straight to bed without saying one word to me. He died a few days later."

"What did the man do? What did our mom do?"

"Neither one did anything. Well, mom cried, but the man just walked slowly back to his house and went inside. I never saw him again."

"Where were our sisters and me when this happened?"

"You guys were all in our house, I think. Our older sister was washing dishes, and our other sister and you were playing on the floor as best I remember," he recalled.

"For the longest time I blamed myself for all of us being separated. I never said much about it until one day at school, I got into trouble for throwing spit wads in class. I was sent to the principal's office. When the principal asked why I was throwing objects in class, I told him I just wanted the police to come and take me back home to where I used to live before I was adopted. When the principal heard that, he called my new mom and dad and told them everything that had happened. A few days later my parents took me to see a psychiatrist. I had to see the psychiatrist for several, maybe ten, visits. All we did was talk about my past and how I had no control over the events that had happened. I was soon convinced. I realized that it wasn't anything I did that caused the court to do what it did. It was something that just happened: our dad died; our mom was not able to take care of four children; we had to go to live with other people in a new house. That was all there was to it," he concluded.

I related to him my experience of visiting with our sister. He seemed interested and encouraged me to try to stay in touch with her as well. He told me he had met our older sister and that she was planning to come to see me when possible. I think that was the first time I actually felt loved.

"Do you think being adopted is bad?" I implored.

"It could be good or bad; or, it could be neither good nor bad," he proposed. "In the case of our family, adoption wasn't good or bad. It was just the result of bad circumstances and the court doing what it thought was good. Adoption can be bad if the person being adopted is placed with a family that doesn't love them and may abuse the adopted person. Or the same could be said about an adopted person that turns out to be mean and disruptive with the new family. Either way, that would be bad. But, what about a person that's in an orphanage, a boy or girl that has no family except the people operating the orphanage? Most orphanages are overcrowded and do not always have enough food and clothing to give to the children. Because of this, many of the children have to wear clothing that does not fit. Many are undernourished and get sick easily. Some of them die before they are old enough to leave the orphanage. In a case like that, when someone wants to give the children a safe, loving home, adoption is very good."

My brother taught me something. I understood there was nothing that I could do to change my situation; the people I now lived with were kind, loving people; my new parents wanted the best for me; it beat living in an orphanage; and, adoption was part of all those things that don't change, come what may.

My brother and I made many more trips to the "coal bucket" where we talked and grew closer as siblings. He graduated high school and then a year later, joined the Marines. He was in Vietnam from March 1965 through August 1966. He was awarded the Silver Star for bravery.

NINETEEN

It was 1963 and our sophomore school year was in full swing. The football team was undefeated, and there was much talk of a state championship trophy about to be put on display in the school's trophy case. Of course, the team had to win its two remaining regular season games. They then had to play and to win the state championship game against a very formidable foe. At this point in the season, there were only two AAA undefeated teams remaining in the state: our school and Buckhannon High School. However, both of our remaining games were with strong, determined opponents.

Our final game of the season every year was with Gary High School located in the town of Gary. The school's nickname of the "Coaldiggers" was fitting because of the town's proximity to the county's largest coal mines operated by U. S. Steel Corporation. They were our fiercest rival out of all the schools in the area. The two schools had been competing against each other in football for over forty years. The winner of the game each year claimed the coveted beer barrel as its prize. (The story goes that the barrel was chosen as a trophy when prior to the first game played between the two schools, a group of miners gathered near the field were drinking beer dispensed from a wooden beer barrel. Someone suggested the empty barrel be given to the winning school as a reward. The idea caught on and was expanded to have the two schools play for the same barrel each year as a symbol of dominance on the football field. The administrators at both schools embraced the idea, and the tradition was born.) The beer barrel was painted in the winning team's school colors with the score and the date of the game highlighted on the side of the barrel. In keeping with tradition, the trophy was displayed in either the gym or the auditorium of the winning school until the following season's game. The outcome of each year's game determined where the barrel lived for the following twelve months. However, even more important to the students of each school than claiming the beer barrel were the bragging rights of having kicked the other team's ass. Of course, that led to many confrontations at drive-ins, theaters, and other hangout places over the months to come, leading up to the next season's game. Then the cycle started all over again.

Students and faculty were also extremely busy with other extracurricular activities as we entered the month of November. One of the most anticipated of all activities was the upcoming annual school Christmas play with three performances scheduled for the first week in December. The cast was always made up of students from all four of the high school grades. The practice sessions were held in the school auditorium three nights each week and on Saturday afternoons beginning the first week in October.

This particular year, Eddie and Robin tried out for parts in the play. Both secured leading roles in the popular Charles Dickens' story of "Scrooge." Hank Preston also auditioned for a part and was chosen for one of the minor, non-speaking characters. He wasn't real happy with the choice, but stuck with it because he still had a crush on Robin. He and Eddie had not yet butted heads over Robin, but the war of words and innuendoes were gaining momentum. All of us had grown in size and hopefully matured somewhat from our first encounters of the seventh grade. Size was one factor that would play an important part in the upcoming clash of the Titans. Eddie was no longer shorter or thinner than Hank. Over the last three years, Eddie actually passed Hank in height by almost an inch and their weight was about equal. But Hank carried that Missouri attitude of show me, and little did he know that he was about to be given a large size can of whoop-ass from an unexpected source.

It all started innocently enough one night at play practice when Hank and Robin were standing next to each other during a break in the action. Mr. Lewis, the play's director and one of the senior class English teachers, was working with Eddie on the presentation of a couple of his lines. Hank started the conversation with Robin, at least that's the way it was later explained, by asking if she had ever considered going out with anyone other than Eddie. After all, he insisted, there were other fish in the sea besides the little shrimp she was currently dating. Maybe she should try going out with a larger fish to see what she was missing. Robin told him she was not on any fishing expedition and that his approach to the whole matter was not one that would soon win him any affectionate interest from any member of the opposite sex.

Patience was not one of Hank's virtues. He quickly retorted by calling her a bitch and exclaiming he only wanted to take her out to get in her pants and not for much else. Robin countered with it was in his best interest to keep his punk ass mouth shut and to stay as far away from her as possible. Hank (drawing from his self acclaimed vast lexicon) responded by again calling her a bitch. However, this time Eddie happened to be approaching when he heard the "b-word" roll off Hank's tongue. Eddie immediately leaped forward and got in Hank's face with a few choice words of his own.

Hank retaliated by shoving Eddie backwards. Eddie promptly regained his balance and lunged forward sending his right clenched fist toward Hank's surprised face. The blow landed flush on the front of Hank's nose, buckling his legs and sending him crashing to the floor. Blood spilled from his nose and mouth. To everyone's astonishment, Hank remained on the floor. He made no attempt to get up. Mr. Tough Guy was down for the count. He was totally shocked by the swift reaction and power of the younger Eddie's punch. Finally, he picked himself up off the floor and exited the building. He dropped out of the play and slowly retreated from the scene at school. The embarrassment of his abrupt defeat was so devastating to him and his brother, Jackie, that both became obscure individuals throughout their remaining time in high school.

Eddie was a lot like Buddy with one exception. Buddy had more of a foul mouth. But, both were free spirited guys who always stood their ground no matter what odds they faced. But they did it in the right way without being a bully or a showoff. They taught me much about self-reliance. They were just tender-hearted, rough boys that happened to also be very good friends. I miss both of them.

TWENTY

The only thing we really knew about Woody Wilson was that his name wasn't really Woody Wilson. Well, we did know that he was not related to Mr. and Mrs. Wilson, the parents of the twins, Mary and Martha. We knew he walked with a limp because he had one wooden leg. That's why most of the kids and some of the adults called him Woody. Others simply referred to him by his first name, Woodrow. He also had a cat that ran away. I think the cat did return a couple of times. Who knows for sure? I do know he was constantly asking anyone that would listen if they had seen his cat. He could be heard from time to time in the evenings and early mornings yelling from his back porch or patio, "here kitty-kitty, here kitty-kitty, come here you fucking feline." Sometimes as a prank, kids would hide behind some nearby shrubbery in the evening at dusk and meow like a cat just to cajole Woody into calling-out, "kitty-kitty, here kitty-kitty, come here you fuckin' fur ball." We all got a laugh out it.

Woody used a cane to get around. Even though he walked with a shuffle and usually just carried the cane much like a person might hold a rifle when hunting in the woods, he could accelerate to a rather fast pace of skipping if the mood hit him. I remember one night in the middle of summer (this time it wasn't Halloween although it seemed like there was a whole lot of shit that went down in our little community on Halloween every year) when Buddy,

Raymond, and I were lighting firecrackers and throwing them at passing cars. We were hoping that the drivers would think one of their tires had just blown and would stop to check it out. Of course, if they did stop, they would be greeted with a barrage of eggs, water balloons, tomatoes, or anything else we could get our hands on to throw. Fortunately for the drivers, none of them stopped on this particular night and thus survived an onslaught of disaster. That was extremely disappointing to all of us. Raymond suggested we go to Woody's house and toss a few explosives onto his front porch for some excitement. When Woody came out to investigate, he would have to endure the rain of asteroids that had been intended for the automobiles and drivers. Luckily for Woody, the only meteors we were carrying on this particular night were a few rotten apples. There wouldn't be too much of a mess to clean up the following morning. Surely, Woody wouldn't be too upset over that. He was a kid once, wasn't he?

When we arrived at Woody's, the front porch light was turned off. In fact, there wasn't a light on in his house anywhere that we could see. We all had the idea that Woody hated visitors and probably had the lights off to keep potential guests away from his front door. Woody's front porch was only ten or so feet from his chain-link fence that formed the border between his undersized front lawn and the dirt road that faced his house. A firecracker or maybe a more powerful cherry bomb could easily be tossed from the road to the front door or beyond if desired. Instead of launching the missiles from the road, Buddy suggested we sneak around to the back side of Woody's house and look through the kitchen window to see if we could get a peek at what Woody might have sitting around in there. After all, he was a mystery man to most of the people around the community. He was especially intriguing to all of us kids.

Woody had been living in our locality for almost a year. He moved in about eight months after Roy's disappearance and the departure of Roy's family. I believe it was in late May. He purchased the old Jackson house that had been vacant for about two years after ole man Jackson was killed in a coal mining accident, leaving a wife, two college-age kids, and a mother-in-law to make it on Social Security Survivor benefits and a small death benefit check from the coal company. The widow and clan moved shortly after Mr. Jackson was laid to rest. (Where they moved to was not known. No one really gave a shit where it was anyway. They were just gone.) Over time the old house began to look run down and kind of spooky.

Before the new owner moved in (no one knew who the tenant was until the day he arrived), there was a major remodeling, fix-it-up project that took place. The roof and all of the windows were replaced; a large two-story addition was erected on the rear of the structure, including a new kitchen on the lower level; and, oddly enough, the area beneath the house was excavated and a basement constructed with entrances from both inside and outside of the house. The partially underground vault was surrounded on three sides by dirt with dark tinted windows resting just below the first floor's floor joists and about six inches above the surface of the ground. The majority of the work on the basement was actually completed after Woody moved in.

While this make-over was going on, the whole community was abuzz with rhetorical questions such as: who in their right mind would invest so much money into fixing-up that old place? Most thought it would have been more economical to just demolish the quarters and construct a new dwelling. The person responsible for all this change had to be one eccentric son of a bitch.

Then Woody rode into town, squeezed inside a taxi

with one large suitcase and two small ones, an average size box, three or four paper bags stuffed with odds-and-ins, the rubber-tipped cane, and a damn cat. He certainly appeared to be the oddball everyone was looking for. Actually, no one knew what Woody's name was when he first stepped out of his ride. Some of the more inquisitive neighbors living near the Jackson place made a special effort to come out of their abodes to welcome him to the neighborhood. He introduced himself as Woodrow P. Wilson, retired serviceman. He said he was elated to now be a part of the community. No one asked which branch of the service he served in, or why he would choose some small town in the West Virginia coalfields to retire to, or even where he was from. Hell, no one seemed to notice his wooden leg either except one of the ten-year-old Dalton twins who promptly christened Woodrow with the appropriate nickname of "Woody." It stuck.

The three of us approached the gate opening to Woody's front yard. After taking one more look around, Buddy unhooked the latch and slowly pushed the gate open. The hinges shrieked a high pitch sound loud enough to wake the dead, but the noise didn't appear to arouse any of the neighbors or anyone inside of Woody's domain. Once inside, the three of us followed the concrete sidewalk that forked near the front porch steps to the left and continued on the right to the rear of the house. The walkway was lined with tall pine trees spaced about ten feet apart. They provided shade during the day, but darkened the area at night. It was the perfect cover from the light of the moon, and we were able to travel over the entire distance without incident and with no shadows.

A stone patio extended from the smoothly finished cement back porch and ended with its extreme edge joined to the base of a stone and brick wall about twenty feet from the rear of the house. The wall was approximately three feet high with a row of neatly trimmed hedges and flowers lining the wall's border along the top. From behind the shrubbery, we were at the perfect elevation to look directly in through one of two kitchen windows. This particular window was over the kitchen sink where Woody had a panoramic view of the backyard during the day. I imagined him standing there drinking a glass of water and seeing us guys trying to hide ourselves in the undergrowth surrounding the rear edge of his property, making those silly cat calling sounds. From that vantage point, I could tell there was no real concealment in those weeds at twilight.

There did not appear to be anyone in the house. Either that or Woody had gone to bed early. With the possibility of the latter, we knew that movements had to be carried out with caution for our presence not to be detected. The three of us decided to get a closer look through the window. We jumped over the hedges and landed on the stone floor. Our tennis shoes provided a rather soft, quiet cushioning to our fall. Once we were positioned in front of the window pane, we could see a glow of light originating from an area beyond the kitchen. It appeared to be a small night light in the living room. The light was plugged into a wall socket above a wooden table situated against the wall. Over one half of the table's surface was covered with, what looked like, objects associated with a chemistry set. There were several vials and test tubes, beakers and a laboratory burner, probably a Bunsen burner with tubing connecting it to a small tank sitting on the floor beneath the table. Also, next to a set of scales and a brush, there were two chemical racks containing several bottles of something. What was this stuff doing in Woody's place? Was he a drug dealer, or something more sinister? These and other questions raced through our heads as we whispered back and forth to each other. One thing was for certain, we had seen enough. It was time to get the "h" out of there.

However, before we had time to move an inch, we were startled by the screeching of the hinges on the front gate. It was probably Woody, but we couldn't be sure. We quickly darted to the top of the wall and over the hedges and waited to see if the intruder went into the house through the front door or ventured to the rear where we laid prostrate on our stomachs. We could hear footsteps coming in our direction. As the figure appeared around the corner of the house and stepped up onto the porch, we could see that it was indeed Woody. Strangely, he paused as he was placing the key into the door and turned to look momentarily at the hedges. It was as though he sensed or smelled our existence. You talk about the urge to pee! Man, I thought I was going to flood the whole patio. It was all I could do to hold it in. I just knew he had our number.

Woody then turned the key and opened the door. To our relief, in a dry sense, he entered through the doorway into the kitchen and maneuvered again to face our location. As the door was leisurely closed, I could have sworn I saw him smile.

TWENTY-ONE

It finally became apparent that Woody was not so weird after all. A little strange, maybe, but that was a matter of opinion. When the weather permitted, he liked to take evening walks around the community. Some of his strolls were long hikes as far away as the ball diamond, even sometimes following the route along the railroad tracks leading across the trestle. He sure was taking a big chance that a train didn't catch him and that wooden leg on the trestle. I don't think he could have hopped fast enough to outrun the choo-choo. But who knows? Woody was full of surprises. While out for his walks, he would stop and chit-chat with anyone he saw outside their homes and who would take the time to be hospitable. Of course, he always inquired about possible sightings of his cat. Woodrow P. Wilson had the gift of gab.

Once in a conversation with my dad, Woody mentioned that he liked to cut hair. He said that at one time he had owned a small barber shop in Ohio, but he had to give it up after losing his leg. He didn't say how he lost his leg and dad had the decency not to probe. It was too hard to stand up for so many hours each day. Gradually, he had to cut back his hours of operation to only a day or so each week. Eventually, his clientele dwindled to almost nothing and he could no longer afford to keep the shop open. He explained that he did not have a license to cut hair in West Virginia, but he would like to cut a few heads from time to time to keep his skills in tone. He would charge far less than the barber's union scale for a cut and would accept only cash. He offered to clip dad's hair for free to prove he could really do it and that he was not just blowing smoke. Dad said that he seemed sincere enough. So, he agreed to give him a try.

It wasn't long after learning of Woody's skills that my dad accompanied by his brother, Dustan, ventured to Woody's house for that first haircut. Dad said that he and my uncle had to be sure that Woody could trim a head of hair without lowering someone's ears before allowing me and my cousin to have our hair cut by the master. Well, old Woodrow didn't do half bad. My mom even remarked that it was the best cut dad had had in ages.

Soon, several of the neighborhood's men and boys were going to Woody for their trims. The price was right and the cut was good, the perfect combination for starting and maintaining a small business. No one needed an appointment. All one needed to do was to show up and Woody would pull a stool from his kitchen, place it on the patio out back, cover the person from the neck down with an old bed sheet, plug in the clippers, and go to work on the head. If it happened to be raining, Woody would move the whole show to the porch underneath the roof. He cut very few heads in the winter. It was just too cold to sit outside. Everyone assumed that the reason Woody never offered to cut hair inside his home was because he didn't want to deal with all of that loose hair floating around and settling on the furniture and carpet. It would just be too difficult to keep the place clean. That was the assumption. To my knowledge, no one ever asked if that was the raison d'être.

One of the things about Woody that made the hair cutting experience unique was his performance as a conversationalist. He liked to ask questions about the history of the neighborhood and about the people, how long they had lived there, and where they had come from. Sometimes people were slightly offended by the personal nature of his inquiries. Dad said he believed Woody asked so many questions because he wanted to keep his customers talking and not interrogating him with the same questions.

On one occasion when my cousin and I had gone for our monthly cut, we had a surprising, and very interesting conversation with Woody. Our parents made sure that my cousin and I accompanied each other for our hair styling when we were not able to go on the same day as our dad's. It's not that they didn't trust Woody. It just seemed like the right thing to do for everyone's peace of mind. Over time, he had learned a lot about us and the other kids of the neighborhood. Woody had grilled us like a police officer or a school principal about what we liked to do for fun, what kind of games we played, who were some of our friends, and so on. We talked about our pets and playing baseball and crossing the trestle to get to the ball field. We had mentioned Roy and how he had vanished and that no new information had come out concerning his whereabouts.

On this particular visit, Woody wanted to discuss more about Roy and what we knew about the circumstances of his evaporation. We told him everything we knew about first hearing of Roy's disappearance, the search efforts and the follow-up by all of us guys who were Roy's best friends, and even about Sister Brooks. Woody told us he had encountered the Sister when out for one of his walks and he thought that the Sister was a little on the strange side. He had also heard the rumor that the Sister had an appetite for dogs and maybe cats. Woody wondered if Brooks had any idea of the location of his cat.

Just the mentioning of his kitty sent Woody into a long explanation on the importance of a cat. He said people could learn a lot from cats. He missed the many discussions he had had with her. She was a great communicator and never argued with him nor ever pretended to be interested in what he had to say when she wasn't. She did however listen to his every word and never said a damn thing. He then apologized for the loose language and moved on describing how his cat developed so gracefully from being a kitten and then less than a year later merged as a mature and wise adult creature, unlike the creatures of the human kind who enter this world with no knowledge or understanding of life and rarely become more experienced with experience. Well, maybe people do become more experienced, but not often do they become wiser.

Woody was quite the philosopher.

TWENTY-TWO

Life in the community was moving along at a customary pace: people going to their workplaces on a routine basis; kids going to school and playing their typical kid-like games after school and on the weekends. For a period of time, things were actually kind of boring. The majority of the adult men and the boys of the immediate area became regular customers of Woody, and with summer approaching, most of the boys opted for a buzz cut. Woody didn't mind giving that kind of a cut. It was fast and easy with no worries about keeping both sides of the head even and trimming the side burns and such.

There were just a few weeks of school remaining before the summer break when one Saturday morning my cousin Seth and I paid a visit to the local barbershop. (My uncle Dustan had been rather nice to me since the episode with the bicycle and his fence. So, Seth and I were more at ease with each other, at least for now.) We went straight to the rear of Woody's house and knocked on the door as we had done many times in the past. We waited for Woody to answer or come to the door. After several minutes and no sign of Woodrow, we knocked for a second time making sure the pounding on the door was long and loud. Again there was no response from inside. We then rushed to the kitchen window and peered in. To our astonishment we were dumbfounded by what we saw. It looked as though the house was empty of furniture. There were a couple of boxes sitting in the middle of the kitchen floor, but that was it. The table that held all of the chemistry instruments and equipment was no longer against the wall in the living room. The place was vacant. Woody had skedaddled.

Seth and I made a mad dash for home. We each informed our moms it appeared Woody was no longer living in the house. My mom was shocked by the news. "When did he leave and why didn't any of us notice that he was moving?" she thought out loud. "I wonder why he left so abruptly and without, as far as we know, revealing to anyone he was leaving?" she continued. "Your dad was just there for a haircut one day last week and he never indicated that Woody had said he was leaving or even considering a move. Well, before we jump to any conclusions, let's see what your dad or uncle Dustan has to say. Maybe they know something and haven't thought to mention it. We'll see."

Later that afternoon after dad and uncle Dusty returned from a morning fishing trip to nearby Berwind Lake, mom and I broke the news to dad. Dad just laughed and said, "What's the big deal? People move out of this community all the time. I am more surprised by Woody's move here in the first place than I am with his leaving."

"So are you saying that you had no idea that he was considering leaving?" mom asked. "Don't you think it bizarre that he would leave so suddenly without saying anything to anybody?"

"Well, no I did not know he was going to move. But at this point, we do not know if he told anyone he was moving or not. He may have said something to someone. At any rate, he probably had a good reason to leave. And, even if he didn't say anything, is it any of our business why he decided to move?"

"No, it isn't any of our business. I know he was a rather private individual, not having many friends or visitors. Well, he did have plenty of customers that would sit and talk with him. He did like to carry on conversations with people when he went on his evening strolls. With that in mind, it just seems odd that he would leave so unexpectedly," mom replied.

"I guess it does appear to be somewhat odd. But before we jump to anymore conclusions that may or may not spawn some sort of mystery about his disappearance, let me ask around to see if anyone has any information regarding Woody's departure. Fair enough?" dad asked.

"Fair enough," mom answered.

Another week passed and the word had spread that Woodrow P. Wilson had bolted for reasons unexplained. Mostly what I heard was people expressing disappointment that there would no longer be any cheap haircuts handed out in our neighborhood. The men and their wives had come to appreciate Woody's skills. Dad spoke to several of the men who utilized Woody's services and learned some interesting facts. There had been a mid-size, dual wheeled panel truck parked next to Woody's house for a couple of days about a week before we noticed he was gone. Dad also remembered seeing the truck only a day or so after he was at Woody's for a cut and had wondered what it was doing there. One of the men that had had his hair cut during the time the truck was there said he saw a man and a young boy around the age of sixteen or seventeen inside Woody's house. They were in the kitchen, but neither one came outside while he was having his hair cut. Woody explained that they were friends from Ohio who had come to pick up some antique furniture they had purchased nearby and had decided to come a day or two early to pay him a visit while in the area. Dad also learned that the night before the truck left Woody's, the basement light was seen on late into the night and the truck was backed up almost against the basement door. There were sounds like something being loaded onto the truck although the neighbor that had seen this activity could not positively say he had seen anything being carried out of Woody's house. It just made sense that if it walked like a duck and quacked like a duck, then it must have been a damn duck.

Dad was not the only amateur detective asking questions. The general public's curiosity with the whole situation had again triggered further discussions about Roy's disappearance and had even brought to light some other events that most of us kids had never before heard. One of those was the story of a kid that went missing about ten years before Roy and was never found. No evidence of his whereabouts was ever uncovered. He too had vanished into thin air. And there was the account of the young twelve year old black girl that was attacked near the railroad tracks around the same time the boy had disappeared. Lucky for her, she was able to break loose and safely run away. She had been out looking for her brother who was playing ball on the schoolyard long after he was supposed to be at home. When she escaped, she ran in the direction of the school and encountered her brother on his way home. When she related what had just happened, he summoned some of the other boys still at the school, and together they all walked the girl and her brother home. No one was seen along the way. The police had refused to investigate because the girl was not able to identify her attacker due to the darkness and the suddenness of the assault. The incident was soon forgotten.

But now, something else had been noticed that turned the investigation in a whole new direction. First, a man that lived a short distance from Sister Brooks reported that the Sister had not been seen for several days. A brief survey of the surrounding neighbors determined that the

Sister had not been observed in the area since about the same time the truck had been spotted at Woody's. A further examination of the Sister's house uncovered the front door ajar and an indication that the Sister had not been there for several days. The entire community was once again experiencing a "days of our lives" moment. The inhabitants of this kibbutz were taking on the characteristics of a real life primetime TV soap opera.

Sam Vargis, the father of Bill and Melvin, felt like things were getting out of hand. All of the talk about disappearances both past and present were making people paranoid. He suggested contacting the police and reporting the community's concerns, and to let the police determine if an official investigation was warranted. Most of the people, including my mom and dad, agreed. Call it fate or just bad luck, but my dad was chosen as the one to contact either the State Police or the Sheriff's Department to convey the community's unease over the recent suspicious occurrences and observations.

With dad's frequent interaction with the State Police through his work as a night watchman at the Board of Education's bus garage, he chose to speak first with them. As he thought, one of the Troopers that knew dad well said that it was the Sheriff's Department that should do any initial investigating. Then he should call in the State Police only if a kidnapping or other crime involving crossing state lines or multiple counties had occurred. That would be the Sheriff's call to make. It took a couple of calls including one final phone call from the Trooper as a favor to dad to get the Sheriff's attention. A deputy met with dad and Mr. Vargis and some of the other men of the community to compile the initial report. The deputy promised to be in touch and to keep everyone informed with the proceedings. As it turned out, he was true to his word, and after several interviews with many of the neighbors (some of them twice) and more than a few days of searching in the area, the Sheriff's interest focused on the whereabouts of Sister Brooks.

The Sister's house had been gone over with a fine-tooth comb by members of law enforcement, some of whom wore white clothing, a one piece garment much like a jumpsuit that covered their entire bodies including goggles protecting their eyes. They looked much like what we kids envisioned as space invaders from another planet. Buddy, Raymond, and I had observed the aliens carrying out white plastic bags filled with something that none of the investigators were willing to discuss. Once they simply told us kids to stay out of the way and not to go near the Sister's house and for sure to "stay the hell out of the house" were their words. They knew we were watching them work with much interest and asked that we immediately report to them or our parents if we saw anyone near the place after they were gone for the day. We were glad to oblige. I guess it made us feel like we were policemen or detectives or something. It did make us feel important.

Soon after that, the Sheriff's visits to the community became less frequent and the investigation seemed to come to a standstill. Dad and Mr. Vargis and others who had followed the circumstances closely soon became too busy with their jobs and chores around the house to keep up with the state of affairs; and, with the summer respite from school nearing an end, Sister Brooks and Woodrow Wilson were all simply forgotten. Then, out of the blue, dad's friend, the State Trooper, saw dad at the bus garage one evening and told him that the Sheriff's office had obtained some information on the location of Woodrow. He said the Sheriff would be setting up a meeting with the community to go over all of the information that they could legally share and to bring everyone up to date on the investigation's progress. The

Trooper told dad that either he or Mr. Vargis would be contacted with a date for the gathering. They could spread the word throughout the town. At last, we were about to get some answers concerning Woodrow P. Wilson.

After a couple of days, dad received a phone call from Mr. Vargis who had been contacted by the Sheriff. The meeting was set for the next Friday night. The only place in the community large enough to have room for a medium to large size group was in the grade school. Although there was no auditorium in the school, there were retractable doors between the third and fifth grade classrooms that could be opened up to accommodate an estimated one hundred to one hundred twenty-five attendees. Dad and Mr. Vargis contacted the school and made arrangements for the assembly.

Finally, Friday evening arrived and the steady flow of bodies made their way into the room. As expected, about one hundred ten people including the Sheriff's department representatives showed-up. After the customary introductions and acknowledgments, the Sheriff got to the point. It seems that Woodrow Wilson's real name, not to the surprise of some folks, was Michael O'Leary. He was a retired detective from the Columbus, Ohio Police Department with over thirty years of distinguished service in law enforcement. When he left our community, he had returned to Columbus.

"Do you have any idea why a retired detective from Ohio would want to move into a small mining town like ours in the first place?" my dad asked.

"That is certainly a legitimate question," answered the Sheriff. "We learned that Mr. O'Leary, alias Woodrow or Woody Wilson, was in fact the brother of Irene Smith who lived in this town a short while ago. Mr. and Mrs. Smith were the parents of Roy Smith, the boy that went missing, and to date, has not been found. That would make

Mr. O'Leary the uncle of Roy," explained the Sheriff.

A buzz swept over the audience as Mr. Vargis asked, "Has anyone from your organization spoken with Woody, I mean, O'Leary regarding all of these circumstances, like the timing of Sister Brooks' disappearance with his leaving? And maybe anything that he may have found out about Roy?"

The Sheriff continued, "Yes, we have interviewed Mr. O'Leary and are satisfied that his decision to move back to Ohio and the timing of his departure are in no way connected to the disappearance of Thomas Brooks or as you know him, Sister Brooks. What we can tell you is this: Mr. O'Leary came here to look into his nephew's case; he chose to remain anonymous to the community and to local law enforcement for personal reasons; to our knowledge and satisfaction, he did not interfere with any investigations nor did he break any laws. He was and is free to move to any place at any time of his choosing. As far as the story on Mr. Brooks is concerned, the investigation remains open as a missing person's case. Until additional evidence or more information regarding his vanishing becomes available, there's not much more any of us can do to solve this mystery. Mr. Brooks has no known living relatives or anyone that might have a clue about where he may be. That is all I have to share with you at this time."

There were a few more questions from the crowd but nothing earth shattering came from them. The meeting adjourned with mixed emotions. We heard only a very small portion of what we all wanted to hear. However, in addition to learning that Woody was a former police officer/detective and why he came to Big Sandy, it was noted that he had cut hair in Ohio for a number of years as a hobby. So, at least some of what Woody told us was true and not make-believe.

The next week while at work, the State Trooper

stopped by to speak to dad. He said that he had heard about the meeting and it was reported that most people were somewhat disappointed. They were expecting to hear more in-depth, specific details about the investigation. Then he asked dad if he wanted to hear more. Of course dad said yes. Who wouldn't? But as a condition to hearing more, dad had to promise on his honor to their friendship that he would not say anything to anyone about what he was about to be told. Dad swore not to say a word.

"The Sheriff had reported to the State Police that the investigation indicated there was a strong suspicion that Mr. O'Leary (Woody) had been in the Sister's house. The evidence was not absolute, but the sheriff believed that Woody had encountered the Sister at some point, maybe during one of his evening walks, and became interested in the Sister's activities and more importantly, what the Sister had in and around his home. So, the Sheriff made the decision to go to Ohio to meet with O'Leary and was informed first hand of the former sleuth's poking around where the Sister lived. However, the detective would not admit to being inside the Sister's house. Woody had heard the stories of the Sister's presence in the area on the night of Roy's disappearance and also of having been seen near the railroad tracks years before at the time the black girl was attacked. He couldn't see it any other way but believe that the Sister was involved in some way in both episodes and maybe others. He also told the Sheriff that after he approached Mr. Brooks and asked him some questions, the Sister became upset and seemed confused or disoriented. He said he watched for Brooks to leave his home over the next few weeks, but he never saw the Sister outside his home again. Mr. O'Leary had further expressed his deep disappointment in the failure of his efforts to find out what had happened to Roy or any evidence that might help to locate Roy. So, he decided to move back to Ohio and that it was best to leave without having to answer a lot of questions from his neighbors."

"What about the lab items or chemistry set the boys saw once inside Woodrow's house? Do you know anything about that?" dad asked.

"Well, when O'Leary was only a few years away from retiring, he became interested in the forensic side of police work. So he dabbled a little, mainly as a hobby, with some of the lab procedures of testing materials and items found at crime scenes. His records indicated that he was pretty good at getting results even if he was only an amateur. Nothing he did with the lab or chemistry thing was ever admissible in court. He did it simply for self-indulgence and gratification. Heck, he enjoyed it so much that he had the whole basement area of his house set-up like a miniature laboratory," the Trooper explained.

"One more question," dad interjected. "What was in those plastic bags the deputies carried out of the Brooks place?"

"Animal bones!" the Trooper exclaimed.

"Let me guess what kind of animal," joked my dad.

Dad kept his word to his State Trooper friend…at least for quite awhile. Just before my deployment to Nam during one of our several talks, he decided to tell me what he had been told by the Trooper. He thought the whole story sounded like another orchestrated cover-up similar to ones rumored about the cases with Flick and Big John from years past. The reasons for the concealments may be different, but the outcomes were all the same. To this day, no one knows what really happened to Roy or Sister Brooks or – the mother of my birth.

TWENTY-THREE

Not everything that happened in our town was tied to some mystery, Halloween, death, or disappearance. There were a lot of good times too - like the wedding of Mary Lynn Cooper and Rocco Rizzo.

All of us kids referred to Rocco as "Rocky" or "RR Rocky Riz." It just had a ring to it. Rocky was an all-State football star from our rival high school, the Gary Coaldiggers. Mary Lynn was a majorette in our high school band. She was about ten years older than me and my friends. We all thought that she was the most beautiful girl in the whole world. And she did have some long, gorgeous legs. Wow. She lived across the road from my house, next door to my cousin, Seth. I had a perfect view from my front porch when she and RR would come in late on Saturday nights from a movie and sit in Rocky's car in front of her house for maybe an hour. The windows would get all steamed up and no one could see anything inside the car. Not long after the car filled with fog, Mary Lynn's mom would turn on the front porch light. Mary Lynn would jump out of the car and hurry to the front door. There she would pause, kiss her hand, and gently blow the kiss to RR as he slowly drove away. Then, before entering her home, she would also blow a kiss in my direction, knowing I was there peeping from the shadows. Even though I remember that as if it happened every weekend, in reality, I only witnessed it maybe three or four times. Most of the time, I was asleep in bed when they returned from a date.

I had had a crush on Mary Lynn, as did most of the guys my age, since I was five years old. When I turned eight, Mary Lynn was in the last half of her senior year of high school. That May the graduation ceremonies were held in the school gym where she received recognition for her many achievements including the supreme honor for excellence in academics. The foremost prize was a twenty-five hundred dollar scholarship that could be applied toward her college tuition expenses at the college or university of her choice. The entire community was extremely proud of her. Everyone was asking where she had decided to go to college and what would she study, medicine or maybe law? No one expected to hear what they were about to be told.

At the conclusion of the festivities, Mary Lynn made the announcement. She and Rocky were going to forego college for now and get married instead. You should have heard the moaning and groaning coming from the small congregation that had formed around Mary Lynn and her family to offer their congratulations on her success and awards. I recall that Mary Lynn's joy suddenly turned to tears at the reaction of her supporters and she asked, "What's the big deal? Haven't you heard of two young people, who happen to be much in love with each other, getting married right out of high school?"

"It's not that," someone said from the crowd. "It's the fact that you are not going to go to college. It seems that all of that hard work you did in high school is all in vain and going to waste."

Mary Lynn explained, "Who said that we were not going to go to college? You must have misunderstood. What I said was that before we go away to college we were going ahead with plans to be married. We want to have the honeymoon we have planned before we begin school.

Rocky has received a football scholarship to the University of Georgia, and I have earned an academic grant to the school's language arts department. I hope to become an interpreter with the United Nations someday."

"Well, all right then. All is forgiven. Let the celebration begin," another voice rang out from the flock. The faces of disappointment reverted to expressions of joy and harmony.

However, my bliss was short lived. Mary Lynn was the Cooper's only child. She used to hug me and kiss me on the cheek and tell me that I was just like a little brother to her. She said that if I wasn't like a brother, she would marry me instead of Rocky. I had a gut feeling that once Mary Lynn went away to Georgia, it would be just like it was with my real mother...we would never set eyes on each other again. That was disappointing to think about.

The women of the community didn't waste any time. The wedding plans were in full swing. Mary Lynn was occupied making decisions on decorations and colors and sending out invitations and such. Mrs. Cooper and others were planning the reception with food and entertainment and all of the other stuff that goes into this sort of event. I was staying busy with Flick, playing and keeping out of the way of the bridge gang bunch, thinking I was pretty much history as far as Mary Lynn was concerned. Then one evening as my family and I were finishing supper, Mary Lynn and her mother came to our front door. Mom invited them in and offered them something to eat and drink. Mrs. Cooper and mom went into the kitchen and sat down at the table while Mary Lynn remained with me in the living room.

"I have something to ask you and it's very important," she said as she pulled me close and gave me a squeeze. "Would you and your friend, Flick, like to be in my wedding? Rocky and I would love for you two to be our ushers."

"Ushers? What are ushers?" I asked.

"Well, the people that are coming in to the wedding are met at the door by the ushers who escort them to a seat. The families of the bride and groom are seated in a special place while the other guests are taken to seats designated for them. We will have a practice session or two, and you will learn exactly what to do. It will be a lot of fun, and I will love you forever for being with me in my wedding. So, will you do it?"

"You bet I will," I exclaimed. How could I say no? I knew that Flick would be excited.

The practice sessions came and went. Flick and I had to be fitted with tuxes that Mr. and Mrs. Cooper paid for. We didn't mind the suits, but the ties were a little too much. However, for Mary Lynn, we would endure.

Since this was to be a traditional form of wedding in a church, a holy place of peace and sanctity, the decorations had to be chosen carefully. Howard's mom pointed out that beautiful church decorations help create a glamorous ambiance for a wedding ceremony. As it turned out, she was right. At her encouragement, Mary Lynn decided on a variety of colors of roses, lilies, tulips, and daisies. Pink was the dominant color choice along with some red and white roses garnishing the church entrance and the archway at the front before the altar. I wondered why there were no orange roses. Colorful daisies, ribbons, and tulle added a creative, cheerful look to the pews along the aisles. Movable columns held attractive floral arrangements near the altar area making the entire atmosphere fascinating and full of fragrance. Candles of various shapes, sizes, and colors in the candelabra near the arch and in the windows on both sides of the church provided a romantic touch that would make Mary Lynn's special day truly memorable.

Mrs. Cooper said that there was an old saying that a

lady should be in the newspaper only three times in her life: when she is born, when she is married, and when she dies. She said that a person may not have too much control over the first and last of those events, but that the newspaper announcement of the wedding was going to be something special for her only daughter. Mary Lynn decided to skip the engagement announcement since the timeframe of the engagement before the wedding was so short anyway.

Mrs. Coop (we shortened her name to that or simply Mrs. "C" sometimes) wanted the newspaper to have a great picture of the bride fully decked out in her gown, veil, and bridal jewelry because as she said, "Even people who do not know you will be looking at your picture, and many of them will read the wedding announcement because that's what they do for fun. I want them to see the most beautiful bride to ever be in this area's newspaper."

It was interesting to observe how dedicated Mrs. Cooper was to making sure her daughter's wedding went off without a hitch. She seemed to be more excited and happy about the whole event than the bride herself. I couldn't help but wonder if my mother missed doing the planning of such a wedding for my sisters. But then again, maybe it's not a mother's affection that's so loyal, maybe it's just foolishness. After all, Mrs. "C" has always had her daughter, without a fight. My mother lost her daughters, without a fight.

The day of the wedding arrived along with some early summer heat. It was the end of June, but it felt more like it was mid-August with high humidity and temperatures near ninety degrees. The local community church had one (only one) window air conditioner that just happened to be broken and could not be repaired or replaced in time for the ceremony. So to help ease the discomfort that was sure to come from the heat and the clothing, the windows in the front and back of the church were opened. Window fans were installed in the two windows in the back. That created a flow of air through the church; and, with the fans located in the rear part of the church, the noise level was relatively low and didn't interfere with hearing the ceremonial dialogue. The people began arriving on time. Flick and I did our thing and led everyone to their seats. One older gentleman I had never seen before remarked that Flick and I looked like two of the Little Rascals. We never asked to which ones he was referring.

At the conclusion of some special singing by one of Mary Lynn's high school girlfriends, RR Rocky Riz and his best man entered through a side door and walked to their assigned spots beneath the arch. Flick and I closed the front doors to the church and took our places in line with the other two guys in front of the altar. The music started to play. The bridesmaids appeared one at a time in the rear of the church cuddling their bright bouquets. They proceeded to slowly march down the aisle just like they had practiced and lined up on the opposite side of the aisle from Rocky and his support troupe.

The music stopped, triggering a brief prelude to the moment that everyone had been anticipating. Then the organist again began to play. The familiar and powerful sounds of Felix Mendelssohn's "The Wedding March" sprung forth from the instrument's pipes bringing everyone to their feet, turning to face the rear of the church. And there she appeared just like her mother had said, "the most beautiful bride to ever be..." Her face was all aglow and her eyes sparkled from behind the thin veil as she took her first step with her dad by her side, their arms interlocked, looking straight ahead. She was preceded by her four-year-old second cousins, twins Sarah and David from Indiana, who sprinkled red and white rose pedals in her path. Some of the pedals were carried above the pews by the air current made by the fans positioned in the rear windows.

It had only been a few short months since I was told about my adoption. My mind began to wonder. I remember asking myself what my birth mother must have thought when she walked down the aisle in her wedding. Was she happy? Was she thinking about having children and along with my dad, raising a family? When her husband died and her children were abducted, did her memorable moment change? I was drawn back to reality when I heard Flick whisper, "I'll be glad when this is all over. This suit is making me itch."

The minister asked, "Who gives this bride to be wed to this man?"

"Her mother and I," responded her father. It wouldn't be long now. The ceremony was in full swing.

After a reading from the Bible, Rocky received the ring from the best man and handed it to the minister. As the minister was saying something about the ring being a circle, he was suddenly interrupted by a shout of "Oh my God" from the audience. A gasp quickly swept over the congregation as we all realized that an object had flown through one of the windows and had landed on the floor behind the minister. He cursorily turned toward the fallen missile when someone yelled, "It's a hornet's nest!"

Most people sat still waiting to see what the wedding party was going to do. But others were not as patient. Several of them quickly jumped up from their seats and headed for the doors. The minister turned back to Rocky and Mary Lynn and spoke so fast that no one really understood what he was saying until the "I pronounce you man and wife." Instead of having them to face the audience and introducing them as the new Mr. and Mrs. Rizzo, he simply and hurriedly said, "Now let's get the hell out of here before we all get stung!" Because Flick and I were so familiar with word games, I think we were the only ones that felt the "sting" of his words.

It was pure pandemonium. Bees were flying everywhere, people screaming with arms flailing and hands swatting at the kamikaze-like aviators anxious to drop their payloads on the hysterical flotilla of human flesh. Fortunately for the wedding party and anyone else heading for the exit using the center aisle, the air currents from the fans kept the bees off to the sides where the majority of the aerial attacks occurred. Flick and I were able to slither through the maze of bodies and be among some of the first folks to make it to the outside of the church. People were exiting through the doors and leaping or being shoved from the stoop. It was one of the funniest scenes that anyone could have ever witnessed in an entire lifetime.

Some of the men circled the church in search of the culprits that had done this dastardly deed. But to everyone's dismay, no one was caught. On the bright side though, no one was seriously injured by the episode and the reception went off without a glitch. The endless string of pictures were taken and all of the gifts were opened and then the inevitable. Rocky and Mary Lynn said their good-byes, waved to the crowd of onlookers, got into their car, and drove off into the future. 'Sometimes it's hard to distinguish the wish from the well, where you tossed the coin and where it fell' (The Wallflowers).

One thing I've come to realize during my short time upon this earth is that people are constantly coming in and going out of your life. Some move in and then without any explanation move out. Graduations, job changes, bank foreclosures, marriages, divorces, fires, death, you name it and one day everything seems normal and the next day the whole world has changed. Mary Lynn had moved on. Even though she promised to stay in touch, I guess she was just too busy with college and marriage to have time to get around to writing or visiting. Her parents retired and moved to Georgia a couple of months after the wedding.

It's really emotional dealing with all of the many known and unknown reasons for the loss of a friend. Right now, I don't have any friends any closer than Dan, Kevin, the Major, and the Sarge. Eventually, we too will have to say our farewells. Oh, I know we'll make the same promises to write, to get back together from time to time to reminisce. Will we really? This whole war, the very reason we are here in the first place, will probably end just like Mary Lynn's wedding – a contemptuous boondoggle.

TWENTY-FOUR

Being adopted by a family doesn't always mean you are going to have a better life than what you would have had with your birth family. That's probably the intent of the adoption process, but it certainly doesn't guarantee wealth or even living above the poverty line. My new family did not have an abundance of material possessions or money. I guess you could say that we were poor. Hell, we were dirt poor. But the poor like to say that what they lack in material things, they make up in quality time with family and sharing more of what little they do have with friends and neighbors just to get by. Bullshit. I heard someone say once that they had been both poor and rich. And, they were sure that rich was better. I have to agree even though I have never had much money. However, I also agree that money cannot buy you happiness. But again, that depends upon the circumstances for that to be a relevant statement. For example, maybe enough money could buy your way out of this shit hole and that may make you happy. But without the money here, happiness is truly a warm gun. To paraphrase whoever first said it, it's almost good just to be alive.

"Wake-up, Corporal, be very still," Major McGee whispered as he gently shook my shoulder. Sleep is something that's hard to come-by. As often as we can, some of us will nap while the remainder keeps the vigil. Obviously I had nodded-off. I must have been out for some time, having dreamed about so many emotional, life-changing events from my childhood. Flashbacks are frequent ordeals for a lot of us these days. As I struggled to open my eyes, I could hear others being awakened from a brief rest, the Major and Sergeant Major were making their way to each man, slithering through the tall grass like a hungry snake on the hunt.

Recon duty doesn't always have defined time constraints attached. You go out searching, confirming, or pinpointing locations, enemy troop movements or encampments, supply trails, or anything of importance that may serve as an advantage for our guys when engaging our adversaries. Most of our activities are at night, traversing mostly off the beaten paths being careful not to give away our position or presence. We've been together on recon missions in and around the DMZ, Dong Ha Mountain, Helicopter Valley, Freedom Hill, Hai Van Pass, Dong Den Mountain, Elephant Valley, and Song Cu De River Valley. The individual mission at hand dictates the direction we go and the distance we travel.

This is our third day on this assignment of patrolling the hills around the Marine base at Khe Sanh, moving from one outpost to another, gathering and reporting information regarding enemy sightings, locations, and activities between here and the Special Forces camp at Lang Vei. There's a lot of shit going on in the area right now.

Our recon team consists of five or sometimes six members: our Patrol Leader, Major Travis McGee from Biloxi, Mississippi; the Assistant Patrol Leader, Sergeant Major Alfonso "Al" Diaz; Sergeant Chi Lao, an Interpreter/Guide; a Primary Radio Operator (RTO), Corporal Dan (the K-bar man); a Tail Man, Kevin (Tail End Charlie); and me, the Point Man. We don't always have an interpreter or guide with us. Whenever Sgt. Lao comes along, we know there's a good possibility that we may be out for several days and behind, or in the middle of, enemy positions. As a matter of fact, many of our missions have been carried out with only five of us.

First or Second Lieutenants usually lead these recon squads. However, the Major requested and was granted permission to lead a recon unit that was capable of both long-range strategic reconnaissance and surveillance and DA (direct action). However, we are not to engage the enemy except in self-defense unless it is crucial to fulfilling the mission.

The Major and Sergeant Major served together in Korea. Both are battle-hardened soldiers that live to serve as Marines and are eager to lead others into danger zones where most men dare not go. They are great leaders. The rest of us are enlisted guys without career ambitions who just want to serve our time and go home, in one piece and breathing. We were all handpicked for this duty because of our observed stamina, agility, and willingness to follow orders without question, even unto death. The training was intense and brutal, but it was all for a reason. After you've done it for a while, you don't want to do anything else, even if the recon survival rate is marginal at best. We've already beaten the odds. We've been together for approximately ten months without any losses. That has to be some kind of record. The only casualties have been minor cuts and abrasions and an occasional rash. We are either damn good at what we do or awful lucky.

"We've got some visitors. Just below us are two of Charlie's finest. Looks like a couple of scouts, recon mission, like us," McGee expounded. Other details of the men's arrival indicated that they had positioned themselves about thirty yards below, obviously watching the same trail we were observing. The Major surmised that their main objective was to watch for reconnaissance action by our forces and report back any suspicious activity to their unit before another push through the area begins.

"Okay, Corporal, time to earn that pay the Uncle's sending home for you each month," Diaz whispered, looking at me with a glimmer of confidence in his eyes. I knew exactly what I had to do. Running point for so long has given me a ghostly ability to remain invisible to snipers, enemy patrols, and even some of the wildlife occasionally encountered. "Each of the two interlopers will be approached by a grunt simultaneously and taken out as swiftly and quietly as possible. The Major believes that the main force is only two or three klicks away and we do not want to alert them to our location," he continued.

I quickly placed a chew of tobacco, Redman brand, in my mouth. You never know when the juice may be needed to sting the little bastard's eyes. There's no such thing as a fair fight. It's only fair when you win and if that requires cussing, biting, spitting, or any other filthy, disgusting, barbaric act, then so be it. I had seen many of those tactics employed by the rough-necks back in Big Sandy while growing up. Man, could those boys fight.

"When each of you reaches his target, wait for my signal, a whistle, like a colinus virginianus, to synchronize your engagement with your antagonists," Sergeant Major Diaz instructed. "That's Latin for a Bobwhite, by the way," he concluded with that crooked smile of his. The Sergeant Major had indicated that he would use two whistle signals: the first to prepare for attack and the second to initiate contact. Diaz preferred the sound of an American bird to that of a native bird such as the Golden-winged Laughingthrush. Just in case the last sound the enemy heard before departing this world was a birdcall, he wanted that sound to be an American birdcall.

The descent began slowly, being careful not to disturb the grass too much as I crawled on my stomach, getting closer to the ground than snake shit. There was a gentle breeze that helped to camouflage the advance. Abruptly, I came to a halt. There was something moving through the grass toward me. "Could it be that NVA bastard? Had he detected my presence and was trying to get to me first?" I whispered in anticipation.

Suddenly, there it was in front of me, about eighteen inches away, staring at me, eyeball to eyeball. "Holy crap! A green tree viper!" I thought. "Don't move a muscle," I softly told myself. The snake had also stopped dead in its tracks. Its head was raised about six to eight inches and slightly arched back in a striking pose, just waiting for me to make the first move. That was good. It hadn't struck yet. The bastard wasn't looking for a fight, just wanted to be on its way. So, how long was he or she going to sit there and try to charm me? I had things to do and couldn't be held-up too long.

After a few seconds, which seemed like forever, I knew that I had to do something. Using my knife was too risky, possibly drawing notice to the commotion and for sure guaranteeing the chance of being bitten. This legless son of Satan was putting a serious hurt on our plans. Then it came to me. I would strike first with the venom in my mouth – chewing tobacco juice. The aim would be directed at the space right between the little green bastard's eyes.

Gently rolling the cud back and forth, from one jaw to the other, an ample supply of the syrup-like sputum was accumulated. It would have to be ejected from the mouth by forcing the creamy liquid between the teeth. Expelling by puckering-up the lips would simply make too much noise. If the spot was missed, it could bring a retaliatory strike. Of course, there was no guarantee that the snake would move along even if the projectile found its mark. However, it was the only option I had.

Ever so slowly, I adjusted my head, positioning my

face squarely in front of the serpent's visage. Tenderly separating my lips, exposing the gritted teeth, I let the brownish mist fly. The reptile flinched indicating that at least some of the spray had landed somewhere on its sensitive body. For a moment, my body tightened, expecting the worst. Then, as hasty as its appearance, the green monster lowered its vaulted head and swiftly disappeared into the grassy sea. What a relief, I was now able to get back to business. I was still about fifteen yards from the subject. The remaining distance was covered unencumbered, keeping a watchful eye, ever mindful of the viper's passing.

Rising only slightly, slowly, I saw the squint-eyed son-of-a-bitch down on his knees, his eyes fixed upon the path below. It's funny how we look at our enemy and make all kinds of racial and ethnic slurs, calling him or her all sorts of derogatory names. Yet, the same race of people that serve on our side are looked upon as simply one of us, not having any feelings of bias toward them at all, at least, not most of the time. But, what the hell, I'm sure they feel the same way about us, Americans, regardless of the color of our skin. It sort of reminds me of Flick and our infamous encounters with the bridge gang. Those assholes still suck.

The first signal divided the humid air. The Sarge could whistle rather well. It was surprisingly melodious: bob-bob-white, bob-bob-white. Quietly moving from a prone position to my feet but remaining crouched, ready to spring, I placed my knife in my right hand. The second whistle rang out, loud and clear. I leaped forward, striking the subject on the right jaw with my left hand. With cat-like quickness, he had turned toward me at the onset of the second whistle. The adrenaline blow was hard and precise, spinning his body to my right. Quickly with one motion, I wrapped my left arm around his neck placing my left hand over his mouth to prevent a scream. There was a violent twist as he struggled desperately to free himself, but it was too late. My right hand guided the blade of the knife to the right-front portion of his neckline and in one smooth movement, plunged the razor sharp metal through the outer tissue, into the throat, severing the esophagus, then out the back, left side of his neck. There was a slight gurgling sound, and then the body went limp as his life poured out upon the earth. I couldn't help but think of the Bible verse, "from ashes to ashes and dust to dust." My mind flashed back to K-bar man's encounter with the sniper gook on our first real mission after arriving in country nearly a year ago. I imagined the smile on his face as he skillfully eliminated the other observer in similar fashion.

I hurriedly searched the victim for maps, paper work of any kind, or anything that might prove valuable or strategic. There was a map with no significant markings. But there was something more interesting to me. It was a photograph located in his vest pocket, near the heart. It was wrinkled and frayed around the edges indicating that it had been resting in its compartment for some time. The black and white picture was of an older male and female, a young girl that looked to be about my age, nineteen, and an infant. Could this be his wife and child posing with his parents or maybe his in-laws? Although it wasn't clear who these people were, I was certain it had to be immediate family. It was then that I realized that my enemy was no different than me or any other American soldier. He too had an inherent longing for the fighting to stop and to go home to be with loved ones and live without fear. I placed the photo in my pocket.

With both targets successfully eliminated, it was imperative for us to dispose of the bodies immediately. If not, the incessant heat would hasten decomposition and soon notify every flesh-eating creature within miles of the offering. We swiftly dug shallow graves with our trusted Kbars and placed each warrior, face down, in their individual tomb. Their weapons were disassembled and buried with its master. However, the ammo was confiscated. The sites were covered with loose grass and other brush to disguise the soil disturbance and hide, for as long as possible, any evidence of our presence in the area.

I questioned the possibility of these men ever finding their way home. In the space of only a few moments, I thought about my position of being adopted and how going home had a disparate meaning for me than that for a traditional family. I reflected on my childhood with my adoptive parents. They had always given their very best to make sure that I was loved and had every opportunity at life they could envision. But even with all of that, there is still an emptiness that lingers and an unsatisfied yearning to know my ancestry, who I really am. I knew what his family was about to experience if and when the body made it home; or, the anguish of uncertainty if listed as M.I.A. (missing in action). Thousands of American families have also been cursed with the same aloneness. Will the killing ever end? I felt sick. To deal with the haunting of the act, I imagined that he was the God-like proxy judge that had decreed the validity of my adoption, legally kidnapping me and forever separating me from my birth mother, sentencing her to a life of certain loneliness and despair. For one brief moment, revenge was a calming remedy.

"Well done, gentlemen. You both did an excellent job," said the Major. "I am going to recommend each of you for a commendation. It took skill and guts to accomplish what you just did. I am proud of each of you."

What had just happened? What had I really accomplished – followed orders, served my country? I didn't think it deserved any medal. If he had not been carrying that picture, maybe my sensitivity might not have been elevated to such a level with the whole episode.

However, if our roles had been reversed, there is no doubt that the VC combatant would have taken my life. After all, I am sure, in his mind I was the reason he could not go home to his family. I guess he was right, but there is no solace in that thought.

"Thank you, sir, but I don't want any special recognition. I just did my job, sir," I replied. The Major did not answer. For a brief moment, my mind journeyed back to the first grade and recalled the soothing words of Ms. Pridemore, searching desperately for some kind of answer – to what, I don't know.

Being adopted has given me an understanding of solitude. It's an emotion, a feeling as strange as it may seem, that doesn't always show on the outward appearance, but it is ubiquitous on the inside.

I don't remember my birth mother: how she looked; her smile; her voice; her touch – nothing at all. But that doesn't negate the fact that I miss her terribly. Now is when recalling just one of her attributes would be so comforting, assurance that everything was going to be all right. Without ever knowing her, there doesn't seem a way to be redeemed.

Back home, before coming here, I was certain that what I had to do was clear. But after all this time now, I have to question what the hell am I doing here? I know there's no certainty of tomorrow and it's sure as hell hard to tell wrong from right; but, one thing that is undeniable: I'd give anything to be with my family tonight.

For now, the little boy, you know, is still alone.

EPILOGUE

It's been forty-plus years since that time in the bush and sixty-plus years since the boy's nocturnal car ride into a whole new life. It's a lifetime, now having lived it, I would not change.

Dan, the K-bar man, is alive and well, living with his wife in Greensboro, North Carolina. Likewise, Kevin, tail end Charlie, lives with his wife and family in Charlotte, North Carolina. We all get together from time to time. Major McGee retired from the Corps in nineteen-sixty-nine and returned to Biloxi. He is now deceased. Sergeant Major Diaz was K.I.A. shortly after Dan, Kevin, and I left Nam. I returned home and married my childhood sweetheart (we met when I was in the fourth grade and she was in third. We both agree that it was love at first sight). We were both nineteen at the time and have matured with poise together. We have our own family of three children and four beautiful grandchildren.

When asked why I chose to write this story, I simply reply that it's to answer the most common adoption question that all adoptee-persons hear: "What does it feel like to be adopted?"

As a child, I had no idea of how to answer that; although, the question seemed to beg for a response, an explicit answer. My reaction for years was generally to either just avoid (ignore) the question or to make-believe it didn't bother me. Later, I would sometimes merely reply,

"I'm fine with it," or, as a budding smart-ass teenager, ask in return, "what's it like not to be?" It took some of life's experiences to teach me that the question really doesn't need an answer. For me, I couldn't explain what it was like because it was the only life I had known. I couldn't compare it to any other.

After I was told of my adoption, there were a multitude of questions that arose that I couldn't seem to get answered. The frustration soon led me to have feelings of being rejected and abandoned. When I looked at my adoptive parents, I didn't see myself looking back. When I saw myself in the mirror, I knew it was me, but who was I, really? There was a piece missing, and I couldn't seem to find it.

Being adopted means different things to different people, and it's not all negative. To some it's a feeling of being unsettled or that something is unfinished and needs to be completed in their life. Some may feel grief over the loss of a relationship with their birth parents and the loss of the cultural and family connections that would have existed with those parents. Yet, to others, the feeling can be a deep sense of gratitude at having been raised by loving adoptive parents instead of a birth mother and family that could never have given the love that was needed. But to all, there are those times when we are made to feel different and out of place, wondering if adoption was the right choice after all.

From the beginning, I tried to suppress most of my feelings when in the company of others. However, the death of Flick was a turning point. I experienced the giving and receiving of compassion and support in a way that I had not known before. The disappearance of Roy helped me to realize the uncertainties of one day to the next.

In the whole scheme of things, the first nineteen years of my life were not a long time. The experiences of

174

childhood and Nam have given me the understanding that there is a time and place for all of God's children to grieve. And, it is good to "feel." I know that it's not only the years that helped to mold me into who I am, but also the people that came in and went out of my life and perhaps more importantly, the ones that stayed.

There is no right or wrong way to experience being adopted. It would be easier, in my opinion, to explain and accept if birth records were not sealed and the adoption process conducted in its entirety with honesty and openness. Nonetheless, it's about living with the knowledge and awareness of having been adopted, acceptance of and adapting to the situation, and distinguishing the difference between what is reality and what is make-believe.

Nevertheless, if you are adopted, you will think about that fact of your life – every single day.

Made in the USA
Lexington, KY
18 January 2015